Full Moon Shadow

Full Moon Shadow

A young adult novel

Barbara Heinsch

Publisher Name: BHeinsch

Full Moon Shadow is a work of fiction. Names, characters, places, and incidents are products of the author's imagination or are used fictitiously. Any resemblance to actual events, locales or persons, living or dead, is entirely coincidental.

ISBN: 979-8-9878390-2-7

Rev. 1 Nov 24, 2024

Cover design by Barbara Heinsch

DEDICATION

This book is dedicated to our grandchildren:
Braydon, Bradley, Jocelyn, Hailey and Sawyer.

ACKNOWLEDGMENTS

Maxwell Hirsch, a youthful friend, agreed to read preliminary chapters of this book. I thought he might tire of the process but he stuck with it through the entire rough draft. This was extremely helpful as, not only did he give me much needed feedback, he provided valuable commentary and encouragement throughout the early stages of this book's development.

Wendy Nelson, a longtime friend, found time in her busy schedule, to read and edit the first official draft. She also provided great feedback and encouraged me in my efforts.

Mike Pitcairn, by husband, liked the idea for this book from the first time I told him about the concept. He encouraged me to go ahead and write the story to see where my idea would lead. He read sections as well as listened to me talk about the characters and plot changes throughout various drafts and rewrites. When the book was ready for the final edit, I was hesitant to ask him to take on this task. But I was in luck as he agreed to be the final editor of the book. Without his support, there is no way this book would have been completed.

Many other friends listened to me talk about the book during various stages of its development. Their thoughtful suggestions helped me fill in and smooth out the book's rough edges.

Josh King, *Giclee King* Owner/Operator, helped with the cover. He was quickly able to take the nightscape full moon photo I took in Pittsburgh, Pennsylvania, and modify it per my cover concept for use as the book cover. I highly recommend his services. Visit his website at: www.gicleekings.com

Thank you all!

ABOUT THE AUTHOR

Barbara Heinsch is a University of California, Davis (UC Davis) graduate with a Bachelor of Science (BS) degree in Environmental Policy Analysis and Planning. She worked as an Environmental Scientist for over 30 years in both the public and private sectors. She and her husband are both retired and live in northern California. They enjoy traveling, camping, reading, and gardening. They also volunteer at local nonprofit organizations and donate to animal welfare, wildlife and nature conservation organizations.

Barbara has written two children's books: *The Neighborhood Elephant* and *The Neighborhood Cats.*

Full Moon Shadow is her first young adult novel.

USEFUL INFORMATION

It is a known fact that the moon rises in the east and sets in the west and a full moon occurs approximately every 29 days.

 In this story, a full moon event is signified by this image and the text is in italics.

CHARACTERS

Main Characters

Matt Adams, 18 yrs. old	Main character
Cedric James (CJ) Peterson, 18 yrs. old	Matt's best friend

Other Characters

Leah Paine (Aunt Leah), died 1/2/2024 at 78 yrs. old	Matt's great aunt, Brenda's aunt
Derek Adams	Matt's father
Brenda Paine-Adams	Matt's mother
Sally Peterson	CJ's mom
Mitch Leary	CJ's step dad
James Peterson, died 2009	CJ's dad
Darla	CJ's girlfriend
Madison (Maddy)	Darla's friend
Stan and Cara White	Leah's neighbors
Elaine Stewart	Leah's neighbor and best friend
Simon, Edward, Jed, Toni, Stacy, and Kim	Matt's other study partners/friends

CHAPTER 1: JANUARY, 2024

Matt

Suddenly I wake up from an unexpected movement down the hallway from my bedroom. Or is it a noise? I stay on my back listening intently, not moving a muscle. But hear nothing. Well, except Kitty snoring softly on my bed by my feet. I look towards the hallway, but can't see anything clearly. Quietly, I get out of bed to have a better view of the hallway. The old hardwood floors in my bedroom cooperate and don't creak. Kitty wakes and sits up watching me. There is a shadow from the moonlight shining through the west-facing bathroom window onto the hallway wall. The shadow is the shape of a door. I've noticed this before but never thought anything about it.

I don't hear any sounds but I think there's something moving. Carefully, I enter the hallway and see what appears to be the palm of a hand on the doorframe of the shadow. I'm no longer concerned about any noise I make and hurry to the shadow and stare at the spot where I saw the hand but it isn't there now. I enter the bathroom and look through the window to see if there's someone outside casting the shadow. No one there, only the full moon bright in the night sky. I look out the window up and down the side yard, then look at the fence between my house and the neighbor's. I try to look over the fence but can't make out anything. As I turn back

Full Moon Shadow

towards the hallway, I very clearly see the silhouette of a hand waving at me inside the shadow, motioning me to come in.

Back in my bedroom, I stuff my feet into my shoes, grab my phone and run outside to have a look around. I put my phone into flashlight mode. As I open the front door, I try to think what might be going on.

Is it a college friend or neighbor pulling a prank? My heart pumping hard, I walk into the side yard next to the bathroom and look on both sides of the fence for footprints. I stand quietly for a while listening if there are nervous friends hiding nearby trying to not give themselves away. Silence. I return to the front yard and look at the cars parked along the street. I don't see any cars that aren't familiar. I walk up and down the street looking for someone hiding in or around the cars or houses. No one. I return to my yard again and walk completely around the house. There's no sign of anyone. As I approach the front door, I stand and listen. I don't hear any sounds coming from inside the house. But still, once inside, I check each room and search everywhere to make sure there isn't anyone hiding.

I enter the bathroom once again and look out the window at the bright moon. When I turn around and see the shadow on the hallway wall, I don't see any hand waving, no movement from inside the shadow at all. Relieved, I go into my bedroom, kick off my shoes, and place my cell phone back on the night stand charger. I climb back into bed and Kitty jumps up beside me. We both settle into bed with Kitty laying by my chest purring. My heart is finally slowing down and I pet Kitty saying, "It must have been my imagination. Let's go back to sleep."

* * *

When my phone alarm wakes me up, I vividly remember the middle of the night events. I shake my head trying to clear it and try not to think about it anymore. After I get dressed, I look around the house and everything seems normal. Well, as normal as things can be now that I'm no longer living in the dorms. When Aunt Leah

2

Full Moon Shadow

died right after New Year's 2024, I had just finished my first quarter at the University of California, Davis (UC Davis). (In case you aren't familiar with the quarter system, there are three ten-week quarters during the school year; fall, winter, and spring quarters. At UC Davis, the fourth quarter is the optional summer quarter.)

Aunt Leah is actually my great aunt as she's my maternal grandmother's sister. My mom's mother died when I was only two years old and Aunt Leah was glad to step in and help when needed. We only see my dad's parents a couple times a year at most since they live in Florida. Aunt Leah got her Masters in Plant Sciences in the early 70s and was a Research Scientist at UC Davis for over 30 years. She taught classes at UC Davis and was a volunteer educator at community events. She was average height, slim build with shoulder length gray hair and clear, gray-blue eyes.

She was 78 years old when she died and had lived in her 1950, two-bedroom house for 30 years. In her will, she left most of her estate, including her Davis home, to my parents, with a suggestion that they might let me live in it while I attend college here. My parents are well off on their own so they weren't in a rush to sell Aunt Leah's house for the income. When they asked if I wanted to do this, at least on a trial basis, I was a bit unsure about living in Aunt Leah's house by myself.

I thought about it for a while, remembering all the good times I've had at Aunt Leah's with her and my family. I also reminded myself that I'm 18 now and an adult. I should be able to handle living on my own. Why not live in a house that provides privacy and space instead of putting up with a cramped dorm room and little privacy? Besides, I'm sure I can find a someone to move in with me if I don't like living alone. So, at least for now, I'm the sole occupant of this creaky old home.

It took about a week for my parents to break my dorm contract and help me move out of the dorm. They replaced Aunt Leah's old bed and mattress and brought my study desk and computer chair from our home in Berkeley. Mom bought a few other things to make the room my own including dark curtains to block out the light so it is easier to sleep late. It definitely feels like my room now, especially after I put up some of my own stuff on the walls.

While the dorms were fun, they were also distracting which made focusing on studying difficult. It is much quieter living here but I miss my best friend, CJ, who was my dorm mate. I first met him in middle school in my home town, Berkeley, California. It didn't take long for the two of us to become good friends. Even at 11, CJ was taller than most of the other kids in our class. He wore his blond hair long and often in a tail even as a kid. His eyebrows are darker than his hair which makes his face interesting. He doesn't say much but his clear, blue eyes seem to draw people in. Maybe that's why, even though he's super smart, he's also cool. He was always into sports as a kid and in high school, he was on the track team. He still loves running. Now CJ is over six foot tall and he still runs several days a week. No wonder CJ seems to always have a girlfriend; never anyone serious though.

The one thing CJ and I have in common is our age, we are both 18 years old and our birthdays are only about a month apart. Other than that, we are very different. I have dark brown eyes and thick brown hair that I have to keep short as otherwise, it is very unruly. My face is kind of broad with an average nose and thick lips. I don't have a lot of facial hair so I don't have to shave every day. I'm only 5' 7" and stocky which makes me look shorter than I am. I'm short in other ways too. My memory is short so I have to study my butt off. My temper is short so I'm not the "cool guy," more the "quick-to-mouth-off guy." As for girls, they don't ever seem to notice me. My parents encouraged me to try sports, join clubs, all sorts of things to find my *thing* as they put it. But I was just not good at anything. Especially sports so I'm definitely not a jock. While I love to whack things like baseballs, volley balls, tennis balls, they don't go where they're supposed to.

When I met CJ in middle school, we didn't have much in common except we both didn't like this set of boys that were bullies. One day, when the bullies were picking on me once again, CJ managed to help me get out of the situation unscathed. Afterwards, we started hanging out and soon discovered we both prefer to be in quiet places. CJ likes anywhere away from large groups of people while I enjoy the quiet of being outside in nature. That's why we started meeting up to visit nature centers and parks and, as we got older, take hiking and camping trips together.

Once I started high school, I finally found something that interested me besides being in nature. I took a speech class and received my first ever easy "A." Encouraged by my teacher, I joined the debate team and found the thing I am good at – debating. So good, I was soon the leader of the high school debate team. My parents are thankful that I learned to channel my strong opinions into a positive path. They especially liked that my debate skills helped me land a scholarship for UC Davis.

* * *

I look at the time and realize I need to hurry. I have a quick bowl of cereal and finish getting myself ready for the day. I'm going to meet up this morning with a few chemistry classmates to study before our afternoon Chemistry midterm. I really need to do well on this exam.

As I finish loading my backpack and close it up, I think about my interaction with dad when I was home on holiday break in December. When I look at my dad, whose name is Derek Adams, I see an older version of myself with similar features. However, he's taller than me by at least three inches. Dad's hair, while still dark brown, is getting some gray in it now and his face and arms are tanned from being outside. He's a general contractor so goes from one job site to another overseeing projects. He works mostly on big commercial projects so he's really busy but he loves his job. He also has a lot of hobbies that get him outside such as tennis, golf, hiking, and biking. He and I used to go hiking and camping every so often when I was growing up. We haven't been for a couple of years though.

Full Moon Shadow

I guess in height, I take after my mom, whose name is Brenda. She's short for a woman at only 5' 2" like I'm short for a guy at only 5' 7." Mom doesn't like outside activities very much but does golf with dad on occasion. She has a pretty face and her brown eyes turn a shade darker when she gets agitated. Her hair is light brown with some blond in it, which she keeps about medium length. She has gained some weight over the years but still looks the same otherwise. She likes to look nice all the time and admits that she doesn't feel "dressed without her face and earrings on." She's a Certified Public Accountant and works for a big firm. She's in charge of her division. It seems to be a high stress job as when she comes home from work, it takes her a while to unwind.

When I think about how my dad is an outside person while my mom is not, I remind myself that opposites attract. I think about this some more and remember, they do both enjoy concerts, museums, and other things like that. And last year, they went on a cruise to Alaska. Maybe they aren't so different after all.

Thinking about my dad again, I remember how he cornered me while I was gathering my dirty clothes when I was last home. "Son, your grades for Fall quarter were not great. Is everything all right?" Dad didn't raise his voice like mom would have while talking about this subject. He did look disappointed and worried though. I shrugged, stayed calm and resumed sorting my clothes into piles for the laundry. When I glanced back; he was still waiting for me to respond. I turned back to meet dad's eyes and told him as honestly as I could, "It's a bit harder than I thought it would be. I'll do better next quarter. Really." At this, dad clapped me on my back, smiling.

After only one quarter at UC Davis, what did he expect? I guess he thinks I would get great grades like I did in high school, no prob. But this is college and so different. I wonder how CJ is doing with his grades? In middle and high school, he never seemed to crack open a book or appear to be stressed about grades or anything for that matter. And when we lived together in the dorms, he seemed to avoid talking about college classes at all.

Full Moon Shadow

*   *   *

After the midterm, Simon, my chemistry lab partner, asks if I want to join him and a few others for pizza. Simon is a few inches taller than me and he's very intense. He has medium length light brown hair and green eyes. I'm really tired from my interrupted night so I make an excuse and head home. I put my bike in the garage and once inside the house, I drop my backpack on the table. I grab a can of soda from the fridge and plop down on the couch. I sit there relaxing, thinking about Aunt Leah. I asked her once why she never married and she said, "I didn't prioritize finding a life partner so it didn't happen; I'm okay with that."

I look around at the house and can just about see her sitting in the recliner across from me. She was always very strong and agile and loved talking about nature and plants. In my mind, I hear her chatting away about her latest plan for the yard, going over all the details, making sure she answered all my questions about the new designs.

Then she would ask about me. She really listened, didn't say much other than to nod or shake her head. The expression in her eyes would let me know she understood my situation. "Well, given the circumstances, you did the best you could." That was as close to criticism she would ever say to me.

Kitty comes in and curls up beside me. She's my first pet. When I moved into this house, I already knew Elaine Stewart, Aunt Leah's next-door neighbor pretty well. She's 65 years old and a widow; her husband died about 15 years ago. She is a large woman with graying red hair, blue eyes, and a very kind heart. Elaine loves to bake and equally likes to share her creations with neighbors and friends. After her husband died, Aunt Leah made a point of reaching out to her since Elaine didn't have family close by. Soon they became very close friends, getting together frequently to play cards, watch movies and go for walks.

Only a week after I moved in, Elaine rang my doorbell to ask if I wanted to adopt a kitten she had been fostering. I'm not too

Full Moon Shadow

surprised as I know that since she retired from her veterinary practice, Elaine volunteers at the local animal shelter. The kitten was silvery gray with a little tuff of white on her chest, and light green eyes that seemed almost translucent. As soon as I began to stoke her head, the tiny kitten started purring. How could I say no? I couldn't decide on a name so she's just Kitty. As I pet her, I find my eyes can't stay open and I think a short nap will be good after my interrupted night.

When I wake up, the house is completely dark. I shiver when I hear the wind blowing and see tree branches swirling outside in the dark sky. I get up to turn on some lights and turn up the thermostat. As I close the front room curtains, my stomach growls and I realize it's way past dinner time. I reach for my phone and am about to place a food order when there's a knock at the door.

Full Moon Shadow

CJ

I can't believe I am already in my second quarter at UC Davis. The first quarter was quite eye opening. It was fun living in the dorm, hanging with Matt, flirting with the girls, and going to parties. Just what you might expect dorm life to be. All that cool stuff got really old fast for me though as I'm used to a lot of alone time. I found myself seeking out quiet spaces to be by myself. That is how I met Darla. She's a second-year student, drop dead gorgeous, with mahogany skin and dark hair she wears in cornrows. Her eyes are brown with flecks of gold in them. She's almost as tall as I am, very curvaceous and athletic. She's from Texas and has a slight twang in her voice that I find rather sexy. We met in the Memorial Union in a quiet reading room that no one hardly uses. Turns out she's like me and needs her quiet time. We have been together ever since. All in all, first quarter was awesome except for my grades.

In high school, I was a 4.0+ student. School was always easy for me. Most of the teachers didn't bother making me do group projects but instead I did them on my own. The reason being was if I was assigned to a group project, the others in the group would not do anything and let me do it all for them. Homework and exams were typically easy for me. That's why now that I'm in college, I am surprised I'm not acing everything. I know I skipped a few classes and was not as consistent with turning in assignments as I could have been. I think that's likely why my grades at the end of the first quarter weren't stellar.

This quarter I will go to all my classes and take all the assignments more seriously. I want to go to grad school so I will need to get my grades up this quarter. I mention this to Darla and she is very supportive and lets me know to ask if I want her help.

Another thing that is great about college is being away from Mitch Leary, my step-dad. He's been horrible to be around lately. He travels a lot for work and when he is home, he starts every evening with a drink and before you know it, he's had too many. Then he says mean things to my mom. Her name is Sally Peterson.

Full Moon Shadow

Mom is a family counselor so when I asked her about Mitch's behavior, she spits out psychology crap about, "...his having a drink and being rude is Mitch's way to let off steam." She tries to assure me that he calms down after being home for a day or two but I can see his behavior is taking its toll on her.

There's one thing this quarter that is going to take some time to get used to: Matt, my best friend since middle school, is no longer my dorm mate. Instead, he's living in a house not far from campus. Ryan, my new dorm mate, is quite different from Matt. He's tall and looks like a football linebacker with broad shoulders. In fact, that's the position he played in high school. We both like football although I prefer to watch it while Ryan likes to play it. Ryan is also less serious about school than Matt and likes to party. Matt has great study habits which is how he got the grades and a scholarship to UC Davis.

I got accepted into several colleges but chose to go UC Davis, same college as Matt. My mom was very pleased I decided to go with a California college. She claimed the reason was that in-state tuition is so much more affordable but I know that she wants me to be close by. I get it, we are really close since my dad died when I was only five years old. I'm not a huge fan of change myself so staying in California and going to the same college as Matt works for me. He's an awesome friend, very loyal and helpful. However, he's very different than I am; he's much more intense.

I remember when Matt and I first became friends. He used to get upset at boys teasing him about being short. Or even worse, when they would give him grief about his weight. He's not fat but solid. Boys in middle school could be pretty relentless and Matt would sometimes end up in fist fights. After school one day, a punk named Jesse and his friends followed Matt, calling him names. When Matt didn't react, Jesse started throwing dirt clods at Matt aiming for his back or head. They rarely made contact but I could see Matt was getting angry and had balled up his fists, ready to turn around and fight. I was taller than Jesse so it was easy for me to

Full Moon Shadow

walk up behind him, grab his fist filled with dirt and squeeze it over his head. The dirt sprinkled down on him before he could react. Of course, Jesse was furious at me but his friends were laughing at him which made him start pushing and punching at them instead. Matt and I were able to walk away while they all rough housed with each other. We have been friends ever since.

* * *

"CJ, catch!" Ryan throws his football to me and I look up just in time to catch it.

"Let's go outside and toss it for a while," Ryan wheedles me to get up. "Come on dude."

I think about it and realize I have been inside quite a while working on my project outline and could use a break.

"Sure, let's go." We grab our jackets and have a fun time goofing around with the football for about an hour.

"There is a party in the dorm across from ours; let's go join them." Ryan wipes sweat from his brow as he tucks the ball under his arm.

I think about my school project but I'm really thirsty so decide a refreshment won't hurt. "Okay, let's go."

When we arrive, there are several people crammed into a dorm room with music playing and lots of beverage choices. Time passes very quickly and it's dark when I get back to my room. I try to study but my head keeps drooping and I end up falling asleep.

The next day, I mention to Darla that my plan to be more focused on school isn't going well. She encourages me to try studying in the library with her. Then she goes on a long monologue, offering other study tips and suggestions. I nod my head while she's going on and on but I'm not listening.

I will have to be more careful what I mention to Darla about my study habits. I know I can pull up my grades without her help.

Full Moon Shadow

Several days later, Darla and I are in the coffee house trying to warm up from a cold day so I get out my iPad to check if my most recent midterm grade is available. It is and I'm horrified.

"What is wrong, CJ?" Darla looks alarmed by the expression on my face.

"I didn't get an A on my midterm." I tell her this through gritted teeth.

"Let me see that." She turns my iPad to face her. "You got a B+, that's not bad."

"But I should have an A! I did all the homework, studied everything, I don't freaking get it!?" I know I have raised my voice as the people in the nearby tables are looking at me.

"Not everyone can get A's." Darla says with a smile and puts her hand on my arm but I back my chair up so I'm out of her reach.

"I'M NOT …." I don't say "everyone" but it doesn't take a genius to know that's what I was about to say.

Darla stands up and starts gathering her things. Then she bends towards me until her face is level with mine. While looking into my eyes, she says in a low, intense and sarcastic voice, "I don't know what your problem is but you *definitely* need help." She takes a deep breath to calm herself and then quietly continues, "Until you can settle down, we are done." She tosses on her pack, grabs her drink, and briskly walks away. In shock, I watch her leave.

Her telling me to settle down has blown me away. I just sit for a long time thinking about what she said. I don't recall anyone EVER telling me to settle down.

Full Moon Shadow

Matt

When I answer the door to see who's there, I see CJ holding a bag of takeout from our favorite Thai restaurant. I open the door wide to let him in and smile broadly. "CJ, good to see you dude. And you brought Thai. Great minds!"

CJ heads to the dining room table saying, "Bro, I'm so glad you're home. We need to catch up." After we devour our food, I decide to tell CJ about my shadow experience from the night before. I'm kind of nervous he will laugh at me.

"Kinda freaky, bro. So definitely not a prank?" CJ states this more than asks but I hear the doubt in his voice. I don't reply and cross my arms in front of my chest and look at him while tapping my foot. He nods and says, "It's starting to rain and the forecast says it will pour all night. So, no moon tonight." I guess he thinks that is enough said on the subject.

"Yep." I get up and pick up our empty plates from the dining room table and head to the kitchen. CJ follows and starts nosing through the fridge.

"Dude, you have nothing to drink, even the milk carton is empty." He tosses it towards the trash and misses. He grabs a paper towel and makes an attempt to clean up the mess looking sheepish.

CJ is just not into neatness, unlike me. "I was going to shop after class but I was too wiped. I will go tomorrow morning."

"I'll crash here tonight and we can go out to breakfast in the morning." He grins at me.

"Great idea and after we eat, I'll go shop to fill my empty fridge." CJ nods, then goes into the living room, grabs the TV remote and jumps onto the couch. I look at him thinking he must sense that I don't want to be alone tonight. Relieved, I sit on the recliner and relax while he flips through the channels looking for something for us to watch. By midnight, CJ is falling asleep on the couch. I grab two blankets from the closet and toss one on him. I stretch out on the recliner with the other blanket and try to sleep but after that long nap this afternoon, I lay awake thinking about Aunt Leah.

She was the only older-generation family I had nearby as dad's parents live in Florida and my gramma died when I was only two. My maternal granddad never married my gramma and moved away before I was born so the family lost contact with him. I visited Aunt Leah a lot when my parents wanted a kid-free weekend. When I got older, I used to ask to go visit her since I had so much fun at her house. She would take me on nature walks, to museums, things like that. She shared her knowledge about nature and plants as much as I was willing to listen. I enjoyed learning and thought it was great to learn about plants. It was even more fun helping her in the yard with planting, learning how to prune, things like that. That is why my major is Plant Sciences.

My dad, being a General Contractor, oversaw renovations to her house not long after she bought it. She had the wall between the kitchen and dining room removed and the entire kitchen and bathroom updated. Nothing extravagant was done in her house, her focus was on efficiency and function. After that, she only concerned herself with general home maintenance as needed and always asked my dad to oversee the work.

Any changes made to her front and back yards though, she either did herself or oversaw any needed construction. On summer mornings, she would tackle the harder work in her south-facing back yard, taking out old, tired plants and replacing them with new, adding paths, planting a vegetable garden, and having her patio rebuilt. Her yard was constantly changing to suit her changing needs and wants. As the day warmed up, she would relax on the covered front porch talking to neighbors as they walked by with their dogs. She kept the front yard simple, with a small lawn, a couple of shade trees and beds filled with flowering shrubs. Often, people would come over to join her on the porch. She would bring out beverages appropriate for the weather as they caught up with

14

neighborhood gossip or talked about their garden successes or problems, bending her ear for advice.

As she got older, she would hire a neighbor or a gardener to help with heavy pruning. When she retired, her colleagues gave her a bird bath that she installed next to her patio. My mom would tease her that she kept that bird bath cleaner than the kitchen sink. Aunt Leah would roll her eyes at this, ignore mom and wink at me. I smile at this memory and soon fall asleep. A few years ago, she asked my dad to replace her backyard vegetable garden with two raised beds. I helped and she was very proud and called them, "The beds that Matty built."

* * *

While CJ and I eat breakfast downtown, I talk about life at Aunt Leah's house; how I'm now doing my own cooking, keeping the house and yard clean, etc. I try to not sound like I'm bragging living in a house. "Also, I'm taking Kitty this afternoon to the vet. Elaine was a vet for thirty years before she retired and she says it's important to keep up with all her shots, and that sort of stuff." CJ doesn't seem that interested in my rambling but I'm used to him being quiet so I continue. "My parents are a bit irritated I took on a pet. Especially mom. She goes on about pet care being expensive. I try to ignore her and last time she mentioned the cost of cat care, I pointed out that it's nice to have Kitty for company so she stopped complaining."

CJ finally contributes to the conversation and says "You're more outgoing than I am so I would think you might miss the dorm life."

I look at him a bit surprised that he noticed my loneliness. "Yeah, a bit. I definitely need to work harder at having a social life. That's why it was great you came by with dinner. That gives me an idea. How about I have a party?"

"That's a great idea! I can help plan it if you want!"

Full Moon Shadow

I nod my head thinking about how cool it will be to have an actual *house part-tay!* Neither of us speak for a while as we finish our meal and pay.

As we get up to go, CJ says, "I'm going for a long run this afternoon. Then I need to work on a school project that is more extensive than I expected." I get the impression there is something he's not telling me but I don't push it.

Just as he's about to leave, he tells me he'll go with me to the grocery store. I'm not sure why he wants to come along, but okay. It's weird him shopping with me as I notice he doesn't buy much and is pretty quiet. We say our goodbyes and I head home with my heavy load of groceries. When I get home, I put away the food and then mop the sticky floor thinking about CJ. He seemed a bit off today. I wonder what his new dorm mate is like? I forgot to ask him.

Full Moon Shadow

CJ

The evening after Darla broke up with me, I go over to Matt's to surprise him with our favorite Thai. I am hoping he can help me gain some perspective on my love life, or lack thereof. Before I bring up the subject, Matt tells me about this strange incident he had the night before from the full moon shadow in his hallway. Something about someone in the shadow waving at him. I wonder if he's gotten into smoking pot or something else but I know that Matt would not get into drugs. Maybe it's just his overactive imagination.

I am careful to give a noncommittal response that I hope is supportive but by the look on Matt's face, I can tell he's not feeling pleased. I change the subject to the weather to avoid continuing his train of thought. While I see he's not happy with my redirect, I think about our early middle school years. He used to have very strange dreams and loved to tell me all about them. In one, he dreamt about a guy that had a man's body but feet and tail like a chuckwalla lizard. He called this creature Sam Walla and talked about how it would be cool to have a comic book about him. With his crazy imagination, I can't help thinking Matt might consider switching majors to creative writing. I head into the kitchen to grab some milk to wash down our dinner, and find only a swallow left in the container. Matt's fridge is mostly empty which is very unlike him. He's usually very organized.

Later, I notice how relieved he is at my suggestion that I spend the night. I think about his shadow thing and realize he might be more spooked than I thought. I'm glad I can keep him company even though I asked to stay the night because I don't want to take a chance on running into Darla or having Ryan ask about her. We end up watching *Doctor Who* and other shows we like to poke fun at. I had hoped to bring up about Darla and get his opinion but just can't quite figure out how to put the right spin on it so I say nothing.

Over breakfast the next morning, Matt rambles on about what it's like living in the house by himself. It sounds like it might be a

Full Moon Shadow

double-edged sword to me. I mean, I like my quiet time but I still like having people nearby too. I realize living without housemates must be hard for him. That is why I'm glad he comes up with the idea of a party. That should help him kick-start his social life.

We're about to head our separate ways but I realize I'm still not ready to go back to the dorm. Darla might be there visiting some of her dorm friends and I don't want to run into her. I tell Matt I'll go with him to the grocery store. He looks surprised but nods his head. Once at the store, I find it is very interesting watching how he shops. I can see it takes much more thought when you have cook for yourself. I never have to think about that living in the dorms. I notice Matt chooses things that don't require much cooking, who can blame him? I purchase only a few things and then finally head back to my dorm.

Once there, I decide to go for a run like I said I was going to. I put on my gear and, as I run, I wonder what Darla is doing now. Darn, now I'm thinking about her again. If I apologize to her, I wonder if she will take me back?

My mind wanders back to Matt imagining how he saw a hand waving to him in a shadow. I think it's good I didn't tell him about my crap since he's got his own to deal with right now. I can handle my own situation, I'm sure of it.

CHAPTER 2: FEBRUARY, 2024

Matt

Wow, I've been living in Aunt Leah's house now for almost a month. It's still strange to think of her as gone; she was such an energetic woman and role model for me. She was always in great health till almost two years ago when our family went to visit her for her birthday, August 20, 2022. The plants in her raised beds were all dead. I asked her, "What happened to your vegetable garden?"

"I don't have as much energy as I used to." She looked kind of lost. I didn't say anything but instead I went to talk to mom and explained that I wanted to replace some dead plants in the back yard for Aunt Leah. She smiled, gave me her car keys and some cash. After I did the minor yard work, the yard looked better. Then I noticed the bird bath needed cleaning so I took care of that too.

When we visited on Thanksgiving a couple of months later, Aunt Leah and I sat on her front porch while mom and dad went to the store. When a few neighbors walked by and called out greetings, she didn't reply but only waved at them. She whispered to me, "I'm not sure who that is but it's nice they waved." When I told mom about Aunt Leah not remembering her friend's names, she was shocked and asked her about her health. Aunt Leah admitted that her doctor says she'd been having mini strokes for some time. With that, mom arranged an appointment to go with her to the doctor. When the doctor heard about the extent of her memory loss, he agreed with mom that Aunt Leah needed more care. At first, a day care nurse was hired. Elaine also agreed to help out as needed. When she could, Mom would come to Davis on weekends to check on Aunt Leah. Meanwhile, my parents looked for a nursing home near their house that Aunt Leah found acceptable.

During these few months, the weekend visits consisted of mom and dad going room by room to sort furniture and household items as to what to sell, donate, keep or trash. The last room they looked at was Aunt Leah's office. Mom was pleasantly surprised to find many packed and taped boxes. Aunt Leah explained that soon after she retired, she began to sort through her many books, awards, photos and other things. Her huge antique book case was almost completely empty except for a few books and photo albums. There were several boxes neatly stacked in front of the bookcase. The desk had not been touched though. Mom didn't have the energy at this point to do any more sorting so the office was left it as is.

Aunt Leah moved into the nursing home June 1, 2023 and died just seven months later on Jan 2, 2024. Regretfully, I only visited her once during my Christmas break. I miss her. I enjoy taking care of her house and yard as it makes me feel close to her. Still, living here alone is kind of boring and I miss having people my own age around me. When I lived in the dorms, it took no effort to socialize as there are people everywhere. It was fun but the constant interruptions got irritating. CJ was perfect as a dorm mate because he is so quiet. But after the first few weeks of the quarter, CJ seemed to be off somewhere by himself. Once he met Darla, I saw even less of him.

Now that I'm thinking about it, when he showed up with dinner the other night, he said he wanted to "catch up" but I didn't even ask him about that. Also, he never once mentioned Darla which is unlike him. I wonder what that's all about and I text him. "Hey bro! Let's get together again soon." I watch for the three dots to appear indicating a reply in the works but nothing appears. I figure he's just busy and will get back to me later.

Full Moon Shadow

I look outside at the weather; it is raining yet again. While January was pretty dry, February is making up for it. It has rained almost non-stop this month. Since I live off campus now, I have a longer distance to get to class. Whether I ride my bike or walk, my rain jacket and umbrella protect the top of me but my pants and socks get soaked. In desperation, I look online for some okay-looking rain pants but they are all costly and are more for hiking or skiing. Finally, I purchase a pair of geeky rain pants with suspenders like firefighters' wear. Of course, the only color available is yellow. I don't care.

The rain pants arrive the next day via overnight delivery and again, it is pouring. I don't hesitate and put them on over my jeans and adjust the suspenders. They are miles too long so I grab some scissors and cut them off just enough to cover my socks. I can't resist, take a selfie and send it to CJ before getting out my bike and heading to campus. I get a few funny looks on my way to class, but I'm happy as I'm dry and warm.

After a week or so of rainy weather, I see others wearing similar rain gear. They nod or wave at me; seems I'm a trend setter. Smiling, I pedal on to meet Simon and a few other new friends at the coffee house. I text CJ asking if he wants to join us but don't get a response. Likely with Darla.

"Matt, meet Kim. Kim this is Matt." Simon introduces me to a woman about four inches taller than me with reddish hair, gray eyes and lots of freckles. She is carrying a tote bag that I can see holds a pair of yellow rain pants. I notice that Kim is wearing boots and is dry from head to toe.

"Nice to meet you, Kim." I smile as I look at her and feel my face getting red thinking Simon should have warned me, he was trying to set me up. But then I look at Simon and I'm confused.

"Bro, this is MY girlfriend so don't get all googly-eyed. She wanted to meet the genius that started the firefighter rain pants trend." Simon is scowling at me.

Full Moon Shadow

I look down at my arm holding my sloppily rolled up rain pants and finally, I look up smiling. "That's a good idea to use a plastic tote bag to carry the rain pants in. I think that's going to be the new trend." We all laugh and join the line for coffee.

Full Moon Shadow

CJ

All the rain this month isn't helping me with my disposition at all. I have to smile though when I see Matt riding his bike looking like a firefighter in his yellow get up. I saw the text he sent me of this too and realize, I never answered him. I'll reply later. Meanwhile, Ryan is often wanting me to go do something other than study; party, toss a football, whatever. Here he comes now. "CJ, let's go next door to hang with Rajhi and his friends." He gives me this look that means the friends are female.

"Sorry Ry, can't. Gotta cram for midterms." I'm missing Darla more than I care to admit but I'm not ready to see others yet. And I know if I did, my chances of getting back with Darla wouldn't exist. I tried to apologize to her a few days ago but that didn't go well.

"Forget it, CJ. You act like you are so smart but really, you're not." She says this with her arms crossed in front of her. When she sees the look on my face, she softens. "It's just, you're not who I thought you were." She gives me a brief, friends only, kind of hug. I must look pretty pathetic as she adds, "We can study together if you want." When I don't reply, she gives me an exasperated look and she walks away shaking her head. I can't help but think why do I need anyone's help? I never needed help before.

A few more days go by with me ignoring Ryan's prompts to party while I try to stay focused on my classes. However, when I get back more grades and see no real improvements, I feel confused and kind of defeated. When Ryan comes back to our dorm, I ask him, "What's happening tonight? Ryan fist pumps the air and we head out. I think this is what I need, a night off to relax and not worry so much.

Full Moon Shadow

Matt

It's Saturday and still raining. I head out to run some errands and am pleasantly surprised when the rain stops and the sky clears. I decide to take my time and enjoy hanging downtown for a while. When I get home later, Kitty sneaks outside as soon as I open the door. The poor cat has been cooped up inside a lot due to the bad weather; it's no wonder she snuck out. I put my pack in the house and hang my rain gear over the shower rod in the bathroom. I snap my fingers remembering the tote bag idea from Kim. I find one and put it in my pack so I will have it when needed. Time to hit the books to study for my class tomorrow. When I put away my iPad, I notice it is getting dark outside so I look out for Kitty but don't see her anywhere. I'll check again later.

After I fix myself some food, I start to worry about Kitty. It's now dark outside. Just when I think I will have to go on a hunt for her, I hear her meowing to come in. She is soaked from walking through the wet yard and looks more like a wet rag than the beautiful cat she is. I groan thinking about having to clean a muddy cat. I head to the bathroom to grab a towel and I see the full moon shadow on the hallway wall. I stop and stare at it remembering what happened back in January. But this time, I don't see anything moving in the shadow and am relieved. I clean up Kitty and toss the muddy towel on top of the washer in the garage. We both head to bed where Kitty manages to wiggle her way under the covers to get warm. I stare at the ceiling thinking about CJ. I wonder what's up with him, why he hasn't been in touch. Tomorrow, I will track him down and take him to get a meal somewhere new. We can't always eat Thai. I will let him, *no make him*, talk to me.

Full Moon Shadow

CJ

The next few days go by in a blur as I take on a casual attitude about school, parties, everything. One morning, I wake up and find I'm still dressed in my clothes from the day before. "Morning!" Ryan picks up his pack and looks at me carefully. "Wow, that must have been some party!" He's on his way to an early morning class and closes the door behind him quietly.

I hurry to the toilet to puke. Once I'm done, I take a shower and think about the last couple of weeks. I'm totally messing up. Ryan is usually the one who passes out after a party, not me. And he wasn't even at the party last night. This is bad. I don't want to turn into someone like my step-dad, Mitch, who drinks too much and then uses that as an excuse to be a butt. He's not someone to emulate. I pick up my phone.

"CJ darling, how are you?" Mom tends to gush whenever she talks to me. I guess it's because I'm an only child. I typically cringe at her sappiness, but right now, I am very glad to hear her voice.

"I'm okay." She doesn't say anything and I know she can tell by my voice that I'm not okay. I blurt out "Actually, I'm not okay but I don't know what is wrong with me." I have trouble swallowing with the lump I have in my throat. For about a minute, neither of us say anything but I hear her tapping on her phone.

"CJ, I've just cancelled my appointments for the day. I'm coming to Davis to see you." She hangs up before I can protest but I am really glad she is coming.

While I wait for her to arrive, I think about my mom. Her name is Sally Munsch Peterson. She was about to start her senior year in college when she found out she was pregnant with me. She and my dad, James Peterson, had been dating for over a year. He was older than her, already working as an engineer for a utility company and could easily support a family so she put off finishing college. They had a simple backyard wedding that fall and I was born in the spring. We were very happy but then, when I was just five, my dad was killed in a car accident. Mom was devastated.

Eventually, she recovered enough from her grief and decided it was time to finish her education. She always wanted to be a family counselor so it seemed like this was her time to go for it. It was hard for her with a young child but she did it. Her parents, in-laws, and close friends were very supportive and helped as much as they could. It was a confusing time for me with all the changes that occurred over a short time frame. Slowly, I adjusted to our new life style and enjoyed having more time with my grandparents. I missed my dad a lot though and my mom too since she was so busy with school.

Mom met Mitch a couple of years after she finished college and was working as a family counselor. However, I was a bit miffed whenever she went out with him or had him over to the house. I guess it was because I was used to having her all to myself. But I never told her that I didn't want him around as I saw how happy she was with him. They had a huge wedding the summer before I started middle school, it was a fun party from what I can recall.

Once Mitch moved in with us, I found it was nice to have a guy to talk sports and play ball with at the park. I got used to having a step dad and thought it was kind of nice, at least the first few years. Then, when I started middle school, I met Matt. For the first time, I had a best friend.

* * *

I get a text from mom; she's now in Davis and wants to come to my dorm room. I suggest we meet at a coffee house downtown as I don't want her to see my room or meet my friends. After we get our drinks, we talk for over an hour about what has been happening with my grades, partying, etc.

"I don't get it mom, why is college so hard?"

Full Moon Shadow

She thinks a while before answering. "College is more than obtaining a specific degree or career. It offers you the chance to figure out what direction you want to go in your future. You might be able to go through the motions and get a degree without a clear idea of what you want, but remember, the degree is just part of the learning process. Take the time to find your passion and what it will take to achieve it. Then your education will be worth all the effort."

At first, I think what she said is her typical psychology jargon. But then I think about how animated she was when she went back to college. She would talk about her classes to anyone remotely interested and have college friends over frequently, sometimes to study but often to discuss current events, share ideas, and debate controversial topics. She was thrilled when she got her first internship, got a full-time job and now loves having her own practice.

After a long silence between us, I keep my head down looking at my hands. "I get it, mom, really. I remember how hard you worked to get your degree and I see how happy your career choice has made you. I'm proud of you, mom." I look up at her now, kind of self-conscious after expressing all this to her.

"CJ, thank you." She has tears in her eyes and reaches to put her hand on my arm.

Mom dries her eyes and says, "I know you don't like to share your feelings but you really need someone impartial to talk to and help you figure things out. Please consider talking to a campus counselor; I'm sure they can give you more suggestions than what I can give you." I reluctantly nod my head. "Also, have you been in touch with Matt recently? He has always been such a good friend to you."

I tell her, "I haven't talked to him in a while but I'll get in touch with him soon."

She smiles at this. I walk her to her car.

Full Moon Shadow

"CJ, one other thing." She hesitates before continuing. "I didn't want to tell you this until we finished our other discussion." She pauses and then blurts out, "I asked Mitch to move out."

"That's..." Before I can continue, she holds up her hand to stop me mid-sentence.

"He told me he's sorry he's been such a mess this last year. It turns out his job is downsizing and he's worried that he will be next. But I told him, no way does that excuse his drinking and behavior. He agreed and called his friend George to see if he can stay with him for a short time." She looks at me to see my reaction to this news.

"Mom, you have to take care of YOU. But if you want to give him another chance, I understand." She nods her head and I can tell she's still uncertain.

She looks at me very seriously. I know she's shifted back to thinking about me now instead of her own problems. "I'm glad you called. Call again anytime. That's what moms are for!" She looks me in the eye to make sure I am understanding she means day or night, no matter what. I nod in agreement and give her a long hug. She hugs me back and gives me a kiss on my cheek before she gets in her car to head home.

Full Moon Shadow

Matt

My mom gives me a calendar every Christmas that she makes from a photo app. The top half is filled with colorful photos from family vacations and the lower portion has the traditional days of the month boxes with birthdays and important events filled in. I glance at the calendar today and notice that tonight is a full moon.

Now I'm in bed and staring at the ceiling thinking about the last couple of days. Friday, I had a midterm that was tough. I tried to not stress about it as I had too many other things to take care of. Earlier today, I had hoped to go for a hike or bike ride after my busy week but instead heavy winds followed by buckets of rain kept me inside until late afternoon. When the storm finally ended, I walked out to the front yard to look around. Several neighbors were outside dealing with the mess created by the winds. A couple of smaller trees were leaning sideways with their root balls sticking out of the ground. A large tree had fallen across the street and landed on a car completely crushing it. The wife was taking photos of the demolished car while her husband was on the phone with their insurance agent. Smaller branches littered the sidewalks, streets and yards.

Everyone was helping one another with the cleanup so I pitched in. It felt good working with the neighbors, some of whom I never had actually met before. Some people told me how much they missed Aunt Leah and thanked me for helping with the cleanup. I checked out Elaine's house as she told me she was going to be out of town this week visiting her grandchildren. I didn't see any major damage so I just picked up the branches from her yard, driveway and sidewalk and did the same at my house. Once done, I went home for dinner and a shower.

So now, here I am staring at the ceiling trying to sleep. I keep thinking about my great aunt and the nice things people said about her:

"She helped me design my back yard."

29

Full Moon Shadow

"She took care of my garden when I went on vacation."

"She had great backyard parties." That made me smile. I stop staring at the ceiling and turn onto my side and feel myself slide into sleep.

I'm in my bedroom but there is no roof, instead, only sky. The wind is howling and rain is pouring into my room. I look around for my rain jacket and rain pants. I'm drenched and my bed is too. I remember I left my rain gear in the bathroom and head there with my arm over my face to try to protect it from the blowing rain.

Once in the hallway, the rain and wind stop. I go into the bathroom to grab a towel and dry off my face. Since it's not raining anymore, I don't need my rain gear after all so I hang up the towel and turn around to leave the bathroom. Facing the hallway, I see a shadow on the wall. I stop and stare and see something appear. It seems to be a man's hand, motioning for me to join him. I look towards my bedroom and am surprised to see it is still raining there but not in the hallway. I consider this and think, I might as well investigate the shadow; it can't be any stranger than rain in my bedroom.

I slowly follow the beckoning hand and take a tentative step through the threshold into the shadow. I feel a sensation of warmth surround me once I'm inside the emptiness. It is so dark I can't see anything. I just stand there trying to decide what to do. Suddenly, I feel a hand squeezing my forearm; it is painfully hot. I jerk away as I feel I'm being burned.

I wake up with a start and looked around the room. I'm in my bed, there is a roof over my head and no storm. I look out the bedroom window toward the front of the house and see a full moon and stars. Kitty is still right next to me sound asleep. Slowly, I get up and walk into the hallway. The shadow is still present but there's no one motioning for me to come inside. Through the bathroom window, I can see the moon. No one is outside the bathroom window. As I start to leave the bathroom, I look again at the shadow. I don't see anyone there. Suddenly, I feel very cold and dizzy. As I put out my hand to catch my balance, I touch the shadow's doorframe. It feels very warm.

I hurry back to my room, get into bed and pull the blankets up around me, shivering. I can't get warm and get out of bed to grab another blanket from the closet and add it to my bed. Once under the covers, I still can't get warm and keep thinking about the nightmare. Still chilled, I think, "Should I call someone?" I think about who might I call and what I would say. I realize it will sound unbelievable. It would be best if I put it behind me and get over this myself. But the heat from the shadow doorframe, that HAD TO be real. And my arm where it was squeezed, still burns. Shivering, I sit up briefly, turn on the light on my night stand so I can look at my arm. It looks fine, no burn marks even though it still hurts. I turn out the light and continue to think about this for a long time as I try to stop shivering and get back to sleep. Eventually, I warm up enough that I can sleep.

The next morning, I wake up with a headache and chills. I must be coming down with something. As I think about getting up, my phone vibrates. I look at the screen, press accept call, and sit up in bed. "Mom, is everything okay?" I hope she can't tell from my voice that I'm sick.

"Yes, of course, Matty. I wanted to remind you of your dad's upcoming birthday. Are you still coming on Saturday for his surprise party?"

"Sure mom, I still plan to come. What kind of gift should I get him?"

She sighs. "Well, definitely no gag gifts about turning 50. He would hate that. How about tickets to a concert or sporting event that you could go to together?"

"I'm not sure about that but I'll think of something. See you Saturday." I quickly hang up and rush to the bathroom to throw up. Holding my stomach, I climb back into bed and go back to sleep.

Full Moon Shadow

A few hours later, I am once again awakened by my phone vibrating.

It's Simon texting, "Are you coming to study with us or not?" I think about this for a minute then remember we had agreed to meet to study Sunday night since our Chemistry Lab is first thing Monday morning.

I manage to type "I'm sick. I'm staying home."

Simon replied with an exploding brain emoji to which I reply with 'TTYL.' I groan and go back to sleep. Towards evening, I'm no longer puking and able to hold down some water.

The next day, I feel like I'll live. I shower, eat some toast and make it to Chemistry Lab. When I see Simon before class, he says "Bro, you still look sick. Sorry I was so curt yesterday. We count on your brains for our group."

I think he's kidding and start to give him a smart comeback. But when I see he looks serious, I drop that idea and say, "I thought **you** were the chemistry whizz."

Simon looks as surprised as I felt. "I guess it's a two heads thing. Bro, this class requires a team approach."

"Alright, we can study together again soon, okay?" He nods and slaps me on my shoulder and waves goodbye.

Back to the routine of classes, I put the nightmare out of my mind rationalizing that it was caused by a virus. I'm fine now. I few days later, I realize I haven't heard back from CJ about the selfie or any of the other texts I've been sending him. Even for the cool dude himself, it's been a long time to ghost me. I'm done with classes early today so I decide to call, not text CJ. When he answers, I say in a high-pitched mom voice, *"Dude, where have you been? Are you okay? You haven't returned my texts?"*

Full Moon Shadow

CJ laughs and replies in a whiny, little boy voice. "Mom, *I'm sorry*, just busy!" He laughs again and then says in his normal voice, "Yes, I know I've been missing in action. I have a lot on my mind and could use a talk." CJ is serious now and that's a surprise.

"I have time now. Name the place. I'm buying dinner after we catch up." I meet CJ at the redwood grove at the campus arboretum. We sit down on a picnic bench and get comfortable. I notice CJ looks exhausted. I, for once, don't talk and wait for him to start.

CJ says, "I am not doing well in my classes. Not only that, Darla broke up with me. With the stress of all this, I went to see a campus counselor."

I am blown away and can't think of what to say. CJ never needs to study and always is the cool one. Darla broke up with him? I don't get it. He's the one to break up with girlfriends and they usually stay friends with him afterwards. He must know I'm confused because he continues without me prompting him.

"I might have been at the top of all my classes in high school but college is different, you know? Now I need to study and find I don't quite know how to go about it." I start to laugh but when I see the look on his face, I stop.

"The dorms are too noisy. I go to the library and it's too quiet. I was so frustrated with my grades being not what I want, I got angry with Darla and she yelled at me to, 'Settle!' That blew me away. No one has ever told me to settle before. He takes a breath and turns to look at me. This was quite the monologue from CJ. He's not a man of many words.

"CJ," I start to say. But then I realize I can't think of a single thing to say about their argument. I can see Darla's point but then, I know how CJ can be stubborn about doing things his way. Instead, I reach out and punch him lightly on the shoulder and change the subject. "Was it helpful seeing the campus counselor?" I look sideways at him thinking he might not want to share any details.

Full Moon Shadow

"It was good in that she made me realize I'm not the only one that struggles with the transition to college." He doesn't elaborate even when I allow a long pause to encourage him to say more. So, I tell him about my talk with dad after the first quarter and how I've found study partners from my classes which is helping.

"That sounds.... good. Would it be okay, if I come to one of your study sessions to try it out?" I nod my head and wonder if he'll really show up.

"Dude, now I need your help." He looks at me expectantly. "Can you help me think of a good birthday present for my dad?" We both crack up over this and ride our bikes downtown. After getting a burger followed by a boba tea, we walk towards where we parked our bikes. There is no one around us so I use this time to tell CJ about having the full moon shadow nightmare. He doesn't say anything, he just nods. I'm not thrilled that's his only response. He must think I'm psycho and I'm sorry I mentioned anything.

CJ sees the look on my face and quickly says, "You still haven't had the party at your place."

I think about that and it does sound fun, we both need to unwind after what's been happening. "After finals. Let's do it then."

CJ fist pumps the air saying, "We have a plan." I give him a high five. We walk in silence for a few minutes before he adds, "Hey Matt, regarding your raining-in-the-bedroom nightmare, you always have had very strange dreams. I wouldn't sweat it."

I say nothing for a while. Finally, I manage to say "Okay, yeah. I'm sure it was that."

CHAPTER 3: MARCH, 2024

Matt

CJ is going with me to the surprise party for my dad. We are both looking forward to being home for the weekend but also agree we need to use the train time for studying. "Remind me how many units you're taking this quarter?" I ask CJ after we settle in our seats with a table.

"I dropped two classes so I only have 16 units this quarter." He looks sheepish admitting this. Normally, I would say something sarcastic about his comment but think better of it. Instead, I think about how I try to stay under 16 units each quarter myself, after all the minimum needed to be full time is 12.

We discuss the classes he's having the hardest time in and, not surprisingly, it's the classes with team projects and discussion groups. I wonder if he mentioned this to the campus counselor but decide not to ask him about this. Instead, I just get out my laptop and start studying. He gets busy with his homework too.

* * *

The surprise party for my dad is a huge success, he is totally surprised. He thought he was picking up his friend to go golfing and instead, we all jump out of hiding places and yell "SURPRISE!!" I'm glad I didn't miss this party as it was awesome to see the expression on his face, first of shock, and then joy at seeing all his friends and family there for his 50th birthday.

Now that the party is over, we are relaxing at our house while mom collapses from exhaustion on the couch. Dad gives me a curious look and says, "Hey Matt."

Full Moon Shadow

"What?" I say tentatively. I wonder if he doesn't like the gift certificate to the Davis indoor rock-climbing gymnasium I gave him for his birthday. I've been wanting to try it out ever since I first heard about it.

"I forgot to give you something your Aunt Leah wanted you to have. Come with me." I follow him to his office and watch as he rummages through his bottom desk drawer. He pulls out a large padded envelope with my name on it in Aunt Leah's scrawl and tosses it to me.

"What is this?" I turn it over to look at the seal which is taped shut.

"I don't know. We thought you might know." I can tell dad is waiting for me to open it.

"Wow, I haven't a clue." I feel funny opening this now. I notice dad is stifling a yawn while looking curiously at the padded envelope. We both hear mom snoring in the other room. "I'll open this later." Dad nods and heads off to bed. I put the envelope in my backpack before heading out to meet with CJ and other friends.

It's past 1 am when I get home. The house is quiet and I get to bed as quietly as I can. On Sunday, mom has me run errands for her and dad wants to talk about what I'm learning in my classes. We have a decent discussion with no mention about grades which is okay with me. In fact, I enjoy telling him about the interesting topics the profs talk about and the ideas that come up during class discussions. We both completely forget about the envelope from Aunt Leah.

Full Moon Shadow

CJ

Matt and I have a good time taking the train home and attending his dad's surprise party. His parents are so sweet together, it makes me smile and a little sad wondering what my mom and dad's interactions would have been like had he lived.

After the party, Matt and I meet up with a few others and kick it at a pizza place. We spend the time reminiscing and catching up with who's where, what they're doing, that kind of thing.

I head home about midnight and head into the kitchen. I hear Mom call from her office, "CJ, is that you?" I'm surprised she's not asleep already.

"Yep." I answer back. I hear her join me while my head is in the fridge scrounging for something to eat. I bring out the makings for cheese quesadillas.

"I'll have one too." She watches me prepare one for each of us, looking impressed that I know how to use the stove. We sit at the kitchen counter in silence while we enjoy our late-night snack. I'm wondering what she wants to talk about and wait for her to spit it out.

"Mitch wants us to go to marriage counseling. But I told him, he needs to deal with his drinking problem before I would even consider it."

I feel there's more to the story that she hasn't shared with me so I ask, "What aren't you saying?"

"I let him stay here a couple more days after I came to Davis to see you. By day two, he was drinking again and as nasty as before. He's now staying with George until he can find his own apartment." We let that sit for a while in silence.

"I met with a campus counselor last week." She looks a bit surprised but doesn't say anything. I can tell she wants details but knows better than to ask. "She seemed to think a lot of herself." Mom doesn't speak for quite a while.

Full Moon Shadow

"Well, I think counseling over-confident college freshman requires a bit of bravado, don't you think?" She gives me a wry smile.

"Okay mom!" I try to smile but I'm hurt she would say that to me. As I sit and stew about it, I realize I have been rather full of myself these last few years. After a few minutes of silence, I add, "She did have a few suggestions for me to think about. I also talked to Matt and he had some ideas as well."

Mom nods and pats me on the back encouragingly. "That's good to hear." As she passes me by, she kisses my cheek. "See you in the morning, darling."

* * *

Once back at school, I find Darla and let her know what happened to me, all of it. Even my mom coming, me talking to Matt, everything. We are sitting outside on a warm day enjoying the fact it's not raining. I let her know I'm going to go to one of Matt's study groups. She offers to come along for morale support. "Sure, that would be awesome!" I give her a brief hug. "Can you repeat the study tips you gave me a while back? I will listen this time, I promise." At that, she gives me a hug back and gives me a radiant smile.

Full Moon Shadow

Matt

Monday morning, I start to get my backpack ready to go to class and find the envelope from Aunt Leah. I look at the time and realize I need to hurry so I toss it on the couch to open later. I'm meeting Simon and other study group friends at the coffee house before we go to the library to work on homework. CJ is joining us for coffee so he can meet everyone. When I get to the coffee house, I think about how our study group has grown since our first meeting. Besides Simon and Kim, there are four others I'm just getting to know: Edward, Jed, Toni, and Stacy. While we aren't in all the same classes, we have enough classes in common that we meet up about once a week. When CJ joins us, I'm surprised to see Darla is with him. I guess they're at least friends again.

We all get acquainted before the talk turns to how some of us are struggling with Chemistry. CJ listens to our give and take without saying anything. Darla, however, joins in the discussion. "I had Chemistry last year and I definitely struggled." Everyone is listening very closely to what she has to say. "I went to the TA's office hours a few times, that helped a lot."

Toni, a first year with black hair and long eyelash extensions interjects with a curt tone, "I tried that. My TA was not very helpful and kind of snotty."

Darla replies, "Have you tried the Prof?" We all look at her like she's crazy. "Really, they have office hours too and most profs are more willing to help than you might think."

No one says anything for a while then CJ pipes up. "I went to see my Astronomy Prof yesterday. I needed help to get into a group for a project." Everyone, including me, looks at CJ, not quite taking in what he's saying. "I didn't join any of the groups when they formed at the first of the quarter as I thought I could do it on my own. But once I read the instructions and learned the extent of the project, I realized there is no way it can be done solo."

Everyone seems to be holding their breath waiting for him to continue. "He told me that in the future, I need to get into a group right away when the group project is first mentioned." At this, we all sit back thinking that's the end of the story. However, CJ isn't done. "He asked me to show him my project thus far, which I did. He liked what I did so far and made a few suggestions. He recommended a group that I might talk to and gave me the leader's contact information. He said if they agree for me to join their team, he would approve it." Everyone started talking at once all excited about this enlightenment.

Later, some of us go to the library to work on homework. When Jed has a problem, he's unsure how to solve, he asks the group if anyone can help. This leads to a brief discussion about different ways to solve the problem. Out of the corner of my eye, I look at CJ and see him taking this all in. He starts his own homework and after a while, I notice he's now talking to Edward about a problem. I see Darla notices this too and we both are smiling discreetly behind our books.

*   *   *

That evening, I sit down on the couch and open up the package from Aunt Leah. First thing I take out is her letter.

Full Moon Shadow

Dear Matt,   February 1, 2023

I know you are curious as to why I'm writing you a letter to read after I'm gone. I have to tell someone and I think you are the best person to tell. Since I had my first stroke, my memory isn't what it used to be; it's fragmented into bits and pieces. Let me try to explain what I need help with.

Not too long ago and I found something unusual; that I definitely remember. But I can't remember exactly when, what or where I found this object. I keep thinking it was something that needs dealt with so I really wish I could remember. I've looked in the house but don't recall where I put it. I think it was something I found while someone was doing yard work for me. That is why I left you my garden planning journal hoping that might help. Or perhaps if you look at the yard repair receipts that I kept in the desk, they might give you a clue. I'm not sure, sorry.

You might wonder why I didn't tell your parents all this? I have one definite thing in my head and that is a voice saying, "Ask Matty where he used to dig in the yard. That's the place." You used to use my garden trowel to search for interesting things like shiny rocks and twigs in the back yard. Anything remotely interesting, you'd ask me, where could you put it to keep it safe? I gave you a metal can to use for your treasures. I put this can in a box marked Matt with some other things I thought you might want to have.

Maybe the treasure can might even have a clue to help you find this missing object but I'm not sure. I'm assuming you are living in my house now while going to UC Davis, so I'm hoping you will look for this object in your spare time and then decide how best to deal with it. I don't think what I found is time sensitive but I know it is something that needs to be taken care of, not ignored. Thank you, Matt, for doing this for me.

Please know, I am very proud of you and am glad I got to be around to see the fine man that you've become. I am so glad you enjoy nature and love to be outdoors. I hope you have a fulfilling and happy life.

Love,

Aunt Leah

Full Moon Shadow

I sit and think about her letter for a few minutes, then carefully, I open the padded envelope and pull out her gardening journal. I remember her writing in this over the years. I thumb through it and see it mostly consists of pages that have a top line with a date and location in the yard and below the page title, she divided the page into three columns: "PLANT NAME / DATE HARVESTED / NOTES." At the end of each season, she would draw out a plan for changes she wanted to make in the fall. She would start in pencil and then once the plan was complete, she would go over it in pen with the final design. There are dates at the bottom of each drawing. I look at the most recent ones and don't see anything that stands out.

I read the letter one more time and realize her letter didn't imply there was a rush. I decide it's best I put this all away and look at it after finals when I can really focus on it. I put the journal and the letter back into the padded envelope. Now, where should I keep this safe? I decide her office would be out of the way and besides, I need to look for the box marked with my name when I get time. I put the envelope in the bottom drawer of her desk and close the drawer. While I'm at the desk, I look in the file drawer to see if her yard repairs file is still there. Yep, and it's a thick file. I bet my mom, being an accountant, will be horrified at how stuffed her desk is with old files and receipts.

When I go back into the living room, I plop down on the couch and try to recall digging in her back yard. My memory is horrible and I have no idea. I decide to put it out of my mind for now and go to bed.

Full Moon Shadow

CJ

As the days pass and finals get closer, I realize I'm finally in a groove. The Astronomy team project I'm now part of is unexpectantly a lot of fun. I begin to participate in class discussions with less concern about if what I have to say is right and just go for it. I'm glad to say that no one is critical of ideas, they all talk openly with enthusiasm. It seems that in college, no one laughs at brainstorming ideas. I begin to look forward to my classes instead of just going through the motions.

"Darla, are you able to help me with this question?" She and I are both sitting at a table in the nearly empty coffee house studying. She looks up at me and nods. "Will you go out to dinner with me tonight?" She grins and nods again.

After dinner, we take a long walk and have a great talk. She lets me know more about herself. Her parents met in college during graduate school. "That is where my mom met her best friend, Jasmine Freeman, who's now is an Anthropology professor. They stayed good friends after college. During her visits to our house when I was in high school, I would listen to her talk about her work projects with my parents and was fascinated. I would pester her with questions until mom would make me leave her alone. I'm hoping she will agree to be my major professor when I'm in grad school, that's, if I get accepted to her university."

"Darla, I'm sure she will be glad to be your major professor. You are so focused and know exactly what you want."

She smiles and nods. "What about your plans after graduation?"

I hesitate and then say truthfully, "I'm not sure. I definitely love physics but I have no clear idea what I might do with it for a career. I'm still trying to figure that out. For now, I'm keeping my options open."

She looks me in the eyes and says, "That makes perfect sense." Then she grabs my hand and pulls me away from the busy intersection we were about to cross. She pulls me into a hug and

Full Moon Shadow

when I hug her back, she surprises me with a kiss that says all I need to know.

*   *   *

I bring dinner to Matt's house a few nights later and surprise him with Darla. I'm glad to see he's happy for us. As we plan his party, I think about what a great house this is and how lucky he is to have the peace and quiet. I walk around the house and yard remembering Leah and think about the times I came with Matt for weekend sleepovers. It sure brings back a lot of cool memories. It would be great if he would let me move in with him.

Full Moon Shadow

Matt

The Friday before finals week, the doorbell rings at 5 pm sharp. CJ is at the door with a bag of soft drinks and a grin a mile wide. I was expecting him tonight, we are going to plan the party. But I have no idea why he's smiling and acting so weird.

"Hey Bro!" CJ says and then Darla jumps out from behind him holding a bag of food that smells delicious. They both kind of tumble inside and I close the door.

"You two seem pretty happy." I can't help but notice they can't stop looking at each other.

"We're back together." Darla says in a rush and quickly grabs CJ and kisses him rather passionately right in front of me. The bag of food is dangling precariously from her hand. I quickly grab the bag and take it into the kitchen. I hear them still at it in the other room so I make a bunch of noise as I pull out plates, silverware, napkins and plunk everything down on the table.

"Food is served, mates!" I call to them in my best Australian accent. They join me at the table and CJ sets down the beverages. We fill our plates and select a drink from the bag on the table.

Before we drink, CJ holds up his drink and looks at us both. "To spring quarter being almost OVER!" We clink our drinks together with laughter then enjoy our meal.

After dinner, I clean up as the love birds start lip-locking again. "Hey!" I yell to get their attention. They look up startled. "We need to plan THE PARTY!" They whoop it up and then we discuss plans for a modest but epic party for next Friday, the last day of finals. Darla and CJ leave wrapped up in each other's arms. It was nice to see him so happy but really, get a room dude. Smiling, I collapse on the recliner.

* * *

I meet up a couple of days later with Edward and Jed at the coffee house for a quick lunch between finals. We are all stressed thinking about what finals we've completed and the ones we still have left to take but we really don't want to talk about it. Instead, we discuss what we're planning to do over spring break. They are both staying in Davis and plan to go hiking, maybe even camp, if the weather cooperates. They ask if I want to join them. I agree and we briefly discuss the details.

As we get up to leave, I ask if they plan to come to my party on Friday. They both assure me they'll be there and talk about how much they're looking forward to a house party. As I leave the coffee house, I can't help but notice that my stress level is far less than when I walked in. I take a deep breath and try to shift my focus on my last winter quarter final.

*   *   *

Finals are over and the house is ready for the party! The beverages are in the ice chest on the patio and the kitchen counter is covered with plates and bowls of party munchies. I've cleared the dining room of furniture so people can dance in the open space. I have my party tunes playlist ready with external speakers placed in the dining room. Around 9 pm, friends from the dorms, classes and study groups start arriving at the house. Many bring drinks or snacks to contribute to the party, as well as additional friends. As the night wears on, the house starts to gets crowded so I open up the sliding doors so we can spread out into the back yard patio.

Around 10 pm, Kim, Simon's girlfriend, shows up without him. She tells me that Simon dumped her right before finals. I notice she doesn't seem to be broken up about it. About an hour later, I see her dancing with friends from the study group and laughing up a storm. Later, she comes and finds me. We talk quite a long time about music, hobbies, anything but classes. "Great party, Matt. I like the tunes you are playing." She is standing really close to me and I think it's just because the music is so loud. I take her elbow and lead her out to the patio.

"I'm glad you like this playlist; I put it together for the party." Kim is now standing only inches from me and is saying something but I am not able to focus on her words. Instead, I think about how her hair shines under the patio lights and her earrings move pleasantly as she talks. My throat seems to tighten and I'm at a loss for words. We are so close that I feel a bit uncomfortable and I try to step back but can't because there is someone behind me.

Finally, I find my voice. "Would you like a tour of the yard?"

"Sure, that would be great!" She sets down her drink and I lead her towards the bird bath. Kim takes my hand as we go. I'm surprised but don't pull my hand away.

"My favorite spot in the yard is the swing seat." As we get walk down the brick path towards the swing, she pulls my hand so that I turn toward her. She looks into my eyes expectantly. I put my arms around her waist and I kiss her.

After several minutes go by, we're both startled when we hear CJ calling my name. "Matt, your neighbor wants to talk to you." I pull apart from Kim and I see Elaine, Aunt Leah's neighbor that gave me Kitty, standing there with her arms folded in front of her.

"Matt, I know you are new to the neighborhood but really, we don't do well with loud parties, especially after midnight. Please turn down the music or move inside so we can't hear it so much." She is trying to not sound angry but I note that while she's trying to smile, it looks more like a grimace. I nod and head inside to turn down the music with Kim following behind me.

Not long after I turn the music down, the party breaks up. Now there are only the four of us: CJ, Darla, Kim and I. Kim and I have been inseparable since our kissing session in the back yard. Now we are standing in the kitchen holding hands. We are talking about nothing in particular with many breaks in the conversation for kissing. "I could stay over and help you clean up in the morning." Kim looks into my eyes suggestively. But I am not ready for this step, way too soon for me. When I don't answer her, the look in her eyes changes but I can't decipher what it means. Maybe disappointment mingled with embarrassment, I'm not sure. Before I can say anything, she starts to walk away.

Full Moon Shadow

I blurt out, "I've never had that kind of a relationship before." Kim stops dead and then turns to look at me again in a different sort of way. I wish I knew what these various looks mean, but I'm completely at a loss so I say nothing.

"Matt, it's okay …. I get it. Really!" Then she takes my face in her hands and kisses me in a way that I wish I could do what she had hoped for tonight. But I know I'm not ready and she must know this too as she turns and leaves without another word.

Full Moon Shadow

CJ

I'm ready to celebrate; finals are OVER! What a quarter it has been. Now I'm at Matt's first house party which is quite a success. A lot of friends as well as their friends show up which make the party rather crowded and loud. We are all having a blast; there is plenty of drinks, food and great music. What more can we want for our first ever house party? With that thought, I find Darla and we dance to a few songs together. I really like the slow ones so we can dance very close. Then I see Edward in the living room waving for me to come over to join him. We talk for quite a while when I hear the doorbell. I'm closest so I answer it.

I'm not surprised to find it's Matt's neighbor, Elaine, here to complain about the noise. I tell myself now I know FOR SURE this was a successful party. After all, only lame parties break up before a noise complaint, right?

It takes some time after the music is turned down for people to find their way back inside and then head home. But there are no more knocks on the door with complaints. By 1 am, it is only the four of us left. While Matt and Kim are busy in the kitchen, Darla and I decide to make up the hide-a-bed in the office. It takes us a long while as we first have to move about three dozen boxes so we can open up the hide-a-bed. It is worth the effort though.

* * *

The next day, we are all tired and groggy. Darla leaves early as she's going camping with friends for a few nights. After I see her off, Matt and I talk about how great the party was. We were surprised so many people showed up, way more than we invited, and many brought food and drinks with them. Also, it was great that so many friends liked the tunes and danced. We both laugh remembering the look on Elaine's face when she came over to complain about the noise.

Also, I can't help but tease Matt about him and Kim being together much of the night. "Bro, you and Kim looked tight last night. I thought she might stay over." I can tell by his response that he turned her down. I think Matt was wise. Especially since she just got dumped; rebound romances are often bad news. I tell him that Darla was my first; he seems a bit surprised at this news and definitely uncomfortable with the topic. He changes the subject and says, "You can stay here again tonight if you want CJ."

"Can't, my mom took the week off so we can spend spring break together." Matt looks at me amazed. I explain about her coming to see me and what is going on with her and Mitch. I look at Matt to see how he's taking this news.

Matt shrugs. "Hey, it's good you can be there to support her. Families are important. Tell her I said Hi." We give each other a fist bump and I go get my pack from the back room. As I walk to the train station, I realize I didn't ask Matt what he's doing over the break. I am so lame.

*   *   *

When I arrive home late in Saturday afternoon, my mom greets me at the door smiling. "Welcome home, sweetie." Over an amazing dinner she cooked for the two of us, we talk about our week together and what we can do. With it being spring break, it will be insane no matter where we go and, since neither of us like crowds, we opt to stay local. We start off by watching old movies and playing board games. I can't help but notice it's much more relaxing with Mitch not around.

Full Moon Shadow

Matt

When I wake up the day after the party, I find CJ and Darla have spent the night and are now in the kitchen trying to find coffee. Once I get the coffee going, Darla mutters, "Have you got any aspirin?" We all take a couple with large glasses of water. None of us wants anything other than coffee. Once her mug is empty, Darla grabs her backpack and mumbles, "Great party" in my direction as CJ walks her to the door.

So now it's just CJ and I laying low, getting over our hangovers. We slowly start cleaning up from the party. Later, over a take-out pizza, CJ teases me about my time with Kim last night. I can tell he wants to know if anything happened after everyone left. I try to explain but just say, "Nothing happened, let's leave it at that."

"I was a virgin until I met Darla." When CJ tells me this, I'm a bit surprised. He doesn't usually tell me this kind of thing. After a few minutes, CJ adds, "Kim is on the rebound so it's good she didn't stay." I'm not sure what to say so I don't respond.

As it starts to get dark, I tell CJ that he could stay the night again if he wants to. I'm thinking maybe he'll help me with the Aunt Leah project which I haven't told him about yet. And he might be interested in hiking with Jed, Edward and I, too. However, CJ tells me he's going home to spend time with his mom over spring break. I wasn't expecting that. I was even more surprised when he tells me about his mom coming to Davis to help him. And that she and Mitch are now separated. No wonder he seemed so quiet during our visit home. Just wow.

While CJ goes to his room to pack, I relax on the couch with Kitty on my lap thinking about Cedric James, aka CJ, and his family. His mom named him after her father, Cedric, and CJ's dad, James. He was always just CJ to me. James Peterson was a very successful civil engineer when he was killed in a car accident in 2009. From what CJ told me, his mom was devastated after his dad died.

When I was in high school, Sally confided in me about how hard it was to deal with losing James. She told me that one day, CJ refused to go to kindergarten because she was crying all day long and he didn't want to leave her alone. That's when she realized she started grief counselling and got the help she needed to recover from her loss.

It wasn't long after that when Sally went back to college to finish her BS degree in Psychology and then continued on to get a Master's degree. She's now a family counselor. When CJ told me about this, he admitted it was tough not having her home as much as before. But he was glad she wasn't sad all the time and he enjoyed having his grandparents around more often to babysit him.

I can't recall what his dad looked like even though I've seen his photo hanging in CJ's bedroom many times. I am pretty sure CJ gets his looks from his mom; they both have thick blond hair, darker colored eyebrows, bright blue eyes and great smiles. He's tall and slim like his mom but she's, well, so beautiful she could be a model. Sally calls CJ 'darling' or 'hon' much of the time. Poor guy, but he doesn't seem to mind.

I do know that Sally's current husband, Mitch Leary, is medium height and nice looking. He has dark blond hair, thick eyebrows, a pointed nose, thin lips and a square chin. He can be really nice one minute and the next say sometime sarcastic and snarky. When he does, he scrunches up his face which makes his eyebrows come together and his face turns mean. When no one laughs as his attempt at humor, he laughs and goes back being Mr. Nice Guy. But after seeing Mitch's mean side, I think he's a creep and I don't like the man.

CJ comes out of his room and says goodbye, then heads to catch his train. Now that he's gone, I work for way too long composing what I hope is a casual text to Kim. "I really enjoyed our time together. Hope to see you again soon. I'm staying in Davis over break." I click SEND before I can rewrite it yet again and wait to see if there is a reply. Nothing yet. I put my phone down and look around the room thinking about that last kiss. I stop myself from reliving it once again and stand up.

Full Moon Shadow

* * *

The next day, I wake up to the unexpected sound of pounding rain and heavy winds and groan. The weather forecast of a slight chance of rain for today was way off. I'm disappointed as I know that will cancel the first planned hike of spring break. I check my phone and sure enough, it's canceled. Instead, I guess I will work on trying to sort out the Aunt Leah project. After breakfast, I go to get the padded envelope from her office and find the boxes that previously were stacked neatly in front of the bookcase are now haphazardly placed against the back wall. Darla and CJ's doings. I guess that was the only way there was room to fold out the couch into a bed. There are sleeping bags piled up next to the bed. I decide to wait until later to deal with the bed/boxes issue.

Next, I spend a couple of hours going through Aunt Leah's journal and backyard plans. When I see the rain has stopped, I walk around the soggy back yard, trying to recall details about when I was a kid digging in the dirt. No spot in the yard looks familiar. I have only vague memories of the excitement I felt when I found shiny rocks and interesting pieces of shells. Aunt Leah would admire my find then get down my treasure can so I could add to it. Then she would put the can back on her bookshelf. I remember thinking that since my treasure can sat next to her many awards on her bookcase, my finds must be valuable or she wouldn't have put them there.

I decide a long bike ride would be nice to clear my head. I text Edward and Jed. Edward is free and we meet and bike for a couple of hours. When the clouds get thick again and the rain resumes, we agree to meet later for a movie. He will check with Jed and Stacy to see if they want to join us.

Once home, I fix myself a late lunch and then I'm ready to finally work in Aunt Leah's office. I have to make the bed back into a couch in order to gain access to the boxes. I struggle to get the hide-a-bed folded away. This ancient couch is something I can't wait to get rid of! I grab the sleeping bags to put them away but find Kitty curled up on them fast asleep. I silently groan.

Full Moon Shadow

My phone pings and I see a text from Edward saying Jed will join us at the theater. I open the garage to get my bike and Elaine sees me as she's getting in her car. It is pouring rain still and I must look a site in my rain gear. She honks her horn and when I look up, she's got her window down and calls to me, "Can I give you a ride? I'm on my way to my book club meeting and glad to drop you off." Gratefully, I accept.

After the movie, we grab a burger and talk about the weather forecast for the next few days before we head home. After showering, I put on old sweat pants and a tee-shirt which is my winter sleeping attire. Once I get into bed, Kitty joins me and curls up next to me purring. While I pet Kitty, I think about the text I finally got from Kim after the movie. "I went home for spring break. TTYL." That didn't really tell me anything. But I knew better than to try to text her again. Sighing deeply, I go to sleep.

Full Moon Shadow

CJ

"Mom, I'd like to learn more about cooking. How about you let me help with dinner?" I explain to mom that since Matt is living in a house now, I'm hoping for our regular Friday dinners, he'd let me cook a meal at his house. Matt's cooking isn't much more than what you can make in a dorm room.

"Really? Okay, how about we make some of your favorites this week while you're here?" She sounds really excited about this idea.

"That would be great! Thanks mom. How about we start with that great chili recipe you have? Matt loves it as much as I do."

"You got it, darling!" She's beaming as she starts to pull out ingredients and the cutting board.

Just then, the phone rings. I'm guessing it's Mitch as mom tells me he calls every couple of days. She leaves the kitchen and answers the land line in the den. (I can't believe they still have a land line!). I shamelessly eavesdrop from the doorway. "That's nice. How are the AA meetings going?" Long pause while she listens. "Well, it only works if you go regularly to the meetings." Short pause and I hear the phone receiver being replaced none too gently. She storms out of the den and nearly runs into me. Her face is red and blotchy.

"Are you okay, mom?" She looks about to explode.

She gets control of herself and says, "Every time I think maybe I made a mistake, he calls. Then within 5 minutes, I'm ready to send him the divorce papers."

"You've given him a lot of chances. Whatever you decide, I'm here for you mom. I just don't want to see him hurt you anymore."

She forces a smile and then says, "Let's start that chili!"

Full Moon Shadow

Matt

I wake up thirsty in the early morning hours. Kitty is in my way so I have to move her so I can get out of bed. She wakes up as I do so and follows me into the bathroom. After I get a drink of water, I notice the light of the full moon coming in through the window. It is a calm night so I open the window to let in some fresh air. When I turn around, I am looking right into the shadow of the door on the hallway wall. I see a masculine figure standing there facing me. He is beckoning for me to come. I'm more curious about the person inside the shadow than afraid of him. Still, it doesn't seem real that someone is in a shadow trying to communicate with me so I turn to look out the window to check if it's someone creating the shadow. No one there, only the full moon and slight breeze from the open window.

I turn to face the shadow once again and he's still there. He turns and starts walking away getting smaller as he goes. He stops and turns back to look at me. As he turns, I see his profile very clearly; he has long hair, a wide forehead, a narrow nose and thin lips. He appears to be waiting for me. Thinking there is no way I can really enter the shadow, I put my hand out to touch the hallway wall but my hand goes through it like it's not even there. Inside the wall, my hand feels warmth where the wall should be. I hesitate only for a second and then step completely inside the shadow.

Now inside, I stand completely still. At first, it is so dark, I can't see anything, even my hand right in front of my face. After my eyes to adjust to the darkness, I can make out the man far ahead of me still slowly walking away. He is a well-lit silhouette instead of a dark shadow as when I see him from the bathroom. I notice the light coming from him is shimmering and appears to be the only source of light. I take a step towards him and I feel what seems to be a flat surface beneath my feet; since I can't see where I'm walking, I follow slowly. I am getting closer to him now but he's still far ahead of me. We have been walking for about five minutes and nothing is happening. My curiosity about the

Full Moon Shadow

Shadow Man is waning and I'm beginning to get worried. What is going to happen in here? Where is he leading me?

As I am thinking about if I should turn to head back, I see he has stopped and is now only several feet away from me. I look at him closely and see the trunk of his body is bright, pulsating light while his face and extremities are less bright. The light within his body is generating heat and I start to sweat. He walks closer to me and stops when he's about an arm's length away. It looks as if he is speaking but I can't make out any words. It sounds only like wind coming from his mouth.

Before I can step away from him, he puts his arms around me and I'm encased within his light. I struggle to breathe; the air is stifling and I'm so very hot. I try to pull away but can't move. I yell but my voice sounds like the wind, just like the Shadow Man's. I stop trying to talk but continue to struggle to break free from his grasp. Suddenly, the ground beneath us gives way and we both fall downward into what must be shaft. I feel a combination of heat from his body and the coolness of air rushing by us as we fall for several seconds.

When we land on what feels like soft dirt, he loses his grip on me and I fall onto my hands and knees. I quickly get to my feet coughing from the dust created by the fall. I'm glad I can hear myself cough unlike earlier when I tried to use my voice. I still can't see anything except for the light from the Shadow Man; he's only a few feet away from me. I try to move away from him as I feel nauseous and lightheaded being so close to him. It's like being too close to a fire. My head is swimming and my body feels like it's melting. I keep trying to back away but I can't move quickly enough and I lose consciousness.

I'm not sure how long I was out but when I open my eyes, I don't see the Shadow Man anywhere. I can tell it's nighttime and notice that I'm lying on my back in the same dirt clearing where we landed from the fall. I sit up and look around at my surroundings. The clearing is roughly in the shape of a circle and is about eight feet across. There are trees all around and the sky is cloudy but

Full Moon Shadow

the full moon is still visible. The Shadow Man is sitting on a large fallen tree several yards away from me. He no longer looks like light but more like a shadow of muted grays and tans that are phasing in and out. We both rise to our feet facing each other.

I walk towards him and say, "My name is Matt Adams. Who are you?" He looks at me but says nothing. I am now about six feet away from him and try again. "Where are we?"

He stands up and says a few words in a garbled, hoarse voice I can't understand. He speaks again, this time more clearly. "My name is Leon Hoke. This was my home." He points towards the clearing. "Your people did not show me the respect I deserve. Are you any different?"

I don't know what to say to this. "I have no idea what you're talking about." I look around trying to figure out where I am and if it will be possible for me to get back home. I'm starting to panic. "How do I get back to my home?" Leon Hoke stares hard at me and I can sense that he is filled with disgust and disappointment. There are several moments of silence between us. It seems like he is about to say more but instead, he walks back to the fallen tree and slowly turns again to face me.

He points directly at me and says in a strong, loud voice, "You ask all the wrong questions. You are of no help to me." I sense his frustration but have no idea what to say to him. I just want to get out of here. He puts both arms straight over his head and places his palms together as if pointing to the sky. Just over his head, I see lightning and then hear the crackle of thunder. I don't see the Shadow Man anywhere; he has disappeared! I cover my ears from the noise but continue to watch the angry sky explode above me. I'm afraid I will get struck by the lightning being under the trees so I go back to the clearing and crouch down in the dirt as low as I can. I cover my head with my arms to protect myself. The lightning is so bright, I close my eyes tightly. The storm continues for several minutes, about the same amount of time as when we were walking in the shadow before falling down the shaft.

Full Moon Shadow

Suddenly, it is quiet. I uncover my head and look around. I'm back in the house, sitting on my bathroom floor covered in dirt. I try to stand up but I'm shaking all over. I grab onto the sink for balance but I'm too weak and I fall onto the floor and lose consciousness.

* * *

When I wake up, I'm in my room in my bed. I can tell it's morning but my room is dark since the curtains are closed. I lie on my back thinking about what happened last night. It is fuzzy but it's starting to come back to me. But, the more I remember, the more it doesn't make sense. It HAD to be another nightmare. But why do I feel so very sticky and dirty? Without getting out of bed, I turn on the light at my bedside table and look at myself. My hands, arms, and clothes are covered in dirt. I get up and look at the bed and see it is filthy too.

It couldn't have been a nightmare or I wouldn't be so dirty. I sit on the bed and try to think sensibly. However, there doesn't seem any logic in this situation at all. I'm not sure of what to do. I see my cell phone on the charger so I grab it and take a selfie. I send it via text to CJ. As the minutes go by waiting for a response, I notice my hands are cold and clammy. I'm feeling kind of nauseous as my memory starts to return. I actually went into the shadow! And met the Shadow Man or Leon Hoke if that really is his name that is haunting the house. I realize I need someone to come help me figure out *what am I going to do about it*?! Still no response from CJ so I text the selfie to my mom too.

I sit on the side of the bed and try to remember in detail all that happened last night. The more I think about it and the strangeness of it all, I start to shake uncontrollably. I get back in bed and pull the blanket up around me. I decide I need to write some of these memories down before I forget so I pick up my phone and start making notes. When my phone rings in my hand, I nearly drop it. I see mom's calling me back. I answer and say, "Mom, I need your help."

Full Moon Shadow

CJ

I wake up Monday morning and check my phone. I see I have a couple of missed texts. The first one is from Matt at 8 am this morning. It's a selfie taken in his bedroom. He's covered in dirt and looks like hell. The text reads, "I followed him into the shadow. I need your help."

The next text is from a number I don't recognize from 8:40 am that says, "CJ, this is Matt's mom. He's in some kind of trouble. We're on our way to your mom's house and hoping you can go with us to help him. We want to be on our way ASAP." I glance at my phone and see it's now 9 am and then I hear a knock on the door. Mom answers and I hear the voices of Matt's parents asking for me. I pull on my jeans and run to the door while pulling a shirt over my head. The three of them are talking and Brenda is now showing my mom a photo on her phone; I'm guessing it's the selfie of Matt. My mom gasps and then turns to look at me as I'm now standing next to her in the foyer.

I look at Matt's parents and say briefly, "I'm coming, let me grab my stuff." I run back to my bedroom, gather my things and stuff them into my backpack as quickly as I can. I'm about to leave when I realize I don't have my phone and turn back once again to go get it.

As I'm finally getting in the car, I hear my mom call out, "Wait! I'm coming with you." As she rushes towards the car, I see she has her purse and a canvas bag stuffed with what I'm assuming are overnight things. It is now 9:15 am.

CHAPTER 4: THE DAYS AFTER

CJ

Derek is driving their car in a methodical way, taking care to not break any laws, but once on the freeway, he enters the fast lane. He's in a hurry but trying his best to restrain himself. Everyone in the car is talking at once but in an incoherent fashion more to themselves. I can't handle it any longer and speak loudly so everyone will hear me. "Mrs. Adams" I start to say and then remember she prefers that I call her Brenda now that I'm older. "Brenda, did you talk to Matt or just get a text from him?"

"First, I got a text from him with a selfie he took in his bed and he is covered in dirt. If that wasn't strange enough, from the look on his face, I knew immediately something serious had happened so I called him. When he answered, he didn't say, 'Hello.' His first words were 'Mom, I need your help.' When I asked him what happened, he talked very fast about a guy in a hallway shadow who motioned for him to follow, so he did. Then he said a lot of things that were even crazier than that. None of it made any sense at all. I don't know what has happened to my son." She's drained of all color having told me this and looks like she wants to scream. She turns to her husband and says, "Derek, can't you go any faster?"

Before Derek can reply, I speak up again and explain that Matt has told me about a couple of incidents he had with a shadow in his hallway but I thought he was just imagining it. "When we were kids, Matt was always telling me about his imaginative dreams. I thought maybe he was stressed from school or living alone in Leah's house. I really didn't think this man in the shadow thing was real."

Derek says, "Of course, it isn't real. But something or someone has done something to him. Brenda, I still think you should call the police. They could meet us there at the house!"

I notice Derek is driving a bit erratically now. I'm sitting behind him and lean forward and ask, "Derek, would you like me to take over driving?" He glances in the rearview mirror at me and shakes his head. He takes a deep breath to calm himself and eases off the gas and stops changing lanes sporadically.

Mom breaks the uncomfortable silence. "I came along as I thought since I'm a counselor, I might be able to help."

Brenda turns around to look at mom and says "Yes, that might be helpful." She pauses and then looks at mom and then at me and asks, "Do you think Derek's right? Should we call 9-1-1?"

No one speaks for a while as we think about it. Derek finally says, "No, I take it back, let's not call the police, at least not yet. Sally, I'm glad you came along." While no one is saying it, we are all aware that Matt might have had, or is having, a nervous breakdown.

Brenda says, "I talked to Matt almost an hour ago. I don't like that he's there by himself. I'm going to call and see if Elaine is home and can go sit with Matt. If she thinks he needs immediate medical help or whatever, she can do what is needed." No one disagrees so she pulls out her phone and makes the call. "Elaine is available and will go right away to the house, she has a spare key so she can let herself in." The tension in the car eases knowing that Matt won't be alone while waiting for our arrival.

We arrive at Leah's house about 11 am and park in the driveway. Before we exit the car, we see Elaine on the front porch, she must have been watching for us from the window. Derek tells me quietly, "I will walk around the house and check on things before I go in." I nod and hurry towards the house with mom and Brenda.

Full Moon Shadow

Elaine holds the door open for Brenda who rushes past her into the house to see Matt. Mom and I stay on the porch to talk to Elaine. "Hi Elaine, we've met before. I'm CJ, Matt's friend. This is my mom, Sally Peterson. She's a family counselor."

Elaine shakes her hand and says, "Pleased to meet you. I'm Elaine Stewart; longtime friend of Leah's and I've known the family for years."

Mom nods her head and says, "It was good of you to come over to check on Matt. I came along to provide support for the family and Matt. If you don't mind me asking, I would like to know what condition he was in when you first arrived?"

"He didn't say much but I could see he was in shock – shaking, pale skin, cold. He was typing into his phone but stopped when I arrived. I told him help was on the way. He nodded and tried to type some more but was shaking too badly. I wrapped a blanket around him and offered to call an ambulance or the police. He shook his head and told me no. I told him I would sit with him while he waits for his parents to come and he nodded okay and seemed relieved I was going to stay with him. So, that's what I did; I sat next to him and gave him sips of water till he could hold the glass for himself. When he stopped shaking, I left him briefly to make some hot tea. When I returned, he was in the shower. I used the time to strip the bed and clean up the dirt from the floor a bit. I waited in the living room till I heard the shower turn off and him go into his bedroom. After a few minutes, I knocked and told him I had tea for him."

Elaine pauses to give us a chance to ask questions but when we don't, she continues. "When I entered his room, he looked a lot better. He was in clean clothes, sitting crossed legged on the bed with a blanket around him. He seemed calm and yet introspective. I asked him if he wanted something to eat, but he declined. I thought about asking him what happened but could sense he didn't want to talk and I couldn't bring myself to ask. We just sat and sipped our tea. You arrived just when I finished cleaning up the tea cups."

Full Moon Shadow

I'm anxious to see Matt so I thank Elaine and head into the house. Mom stays outside on the porch with Elaine. When I enter the bedroom, I see both Brenda and Matt are sitting on the side of the bed; she has her arm around him. I notice the stubble on his face, his bloodshot eyes and dazed appearance. He looks up at me and says quietly, "Thanks for coming."

"Of course I came. My mom came too. She's talking to Elaine right now." I put my hand on his shoulder and add, "We're here for you, bro." Matt's eyes look a bit glassy and he uses the back of his hand to wipe them.

He then looks at me and says, "I didn't have my phone with me in the shadow but after I sent that selfie to you both, I wrote down all I can remember." He thrusts his phone at me. I take it but set it down on the night stand.

"Dude, that's great. It would be good though, if first we can hear what happened directly from you." I try my best to sound normal but I'm so uncertain about the state he's in, I'm having trouble knowing how to talk to him. I feel like I'm using a voice that I would with a small child and I know that isn't right.

Matt doesn't seem to notice my tone and says quietly, "I don't think I can tell it more than once. Let's go to the living room." He picks up his phone and puts it in his pocket. Then he stands up but gets woozy and needs to steady himself. He puts his hand on his mom's shoulder and she puts her arm around his waist. He grabs a blanket from his bed with his other hand and tucks it under his arm. The two of them head slowly toward the living room and I follow behind. When they reach the hallway across from the bathroom, Brenda glances back at me as if to ask, 'Is that the place?' I nod yes. Of course, since it's daylight, there is no shadow on the wall but it is a short hallway and we both imagine where the shadow of the door would appear. Brenda seems to shudder a bit as she walks past it.

After Matt makes himself comfortable in the recliner, Derek comes in and goes directly to Matt. He leans over him and puts his hand on his shoulder. They talk softly to one another. Since

Full Moon Shadow

the only other seating in the front room is a couch that fits three, Brenda and I bring in two kitchen chairs and place them on either side of the recliner. She sits in one and Derek sits in the other, both wanting to be next to their son. Before I move to sit on the couch, Brenda whispers to me, "Do you think we should take him to see a doctor?" I shrug my shoulders. I see mom and Elaine are now at the front door.

Elaine knocks briefly before opening the door. She sees Brenda and tells her, "We've got coffee started at my house and will bring it over in a few minutes. Do you want us to bring some sandwiches over too?"

"Thank you, Elaine, we so appreciate your help. Just coffee for now please. Later I'm sure we will want some sandwiches. Also, Matt's getting ready to tell us what happened. You're welcome to join us. You are like family to us, you know." Brenda gives Elaine a weak smile in appreciation.

Elaine smiles back at her but shakes her head and then goes with mom to get the coffee from her house. A few minutes later, they return and serve coffee which everyone gratefully accepts, except Matt. He asks for a glass of water. Mom gets it for him and then takes a seat next to me on the couch. Elaine places the coffee tray on the dining room table then quietly leaves. After the door closes, we all turn to look at Matt.

"Every full moon for the last three months, a man within a shadow has appeared in the hallway waving for me to come in. The first time, I thought it was a college friend playing a prank. The second time, it seemed more of a nightmare than an actual occurrence. I dreamt it was raining in my bedroom and got up to go into the bathroom to get my rain gear. It wasn't raining in the hallway or bathroom and when I saw the man in the shadow, I decided I might as well follow him."

"Once in the shadow, he grabbed my arm and it felt like it was burning me which woke me up. When I tried to go back to sleep, I noticed my arm still hurt from where he grabbed me. I checked my arm and it looked fine. I reasoned it was my imagination and

Full Moon Shadow

eventually was able to go back to sleep. The next day, I had a stomach bug so that convinced me that it had been only a bad dream. However, when the full moon shadow happened yesterday, I found out the Shadow Man is real." There is a pause while we all take in this information.

Brenda starts to tear up and reaches for a tissue. Sally looks at Matt as if trying to determine if he's lucid. Derek looks at Sally and then back at Matt. I try to gauge how I feel about it. It's so unbelievable but from the sincere tone in Matt's voice, I have a hard time thinking he's ready for a psych ward.

"I know you think I'm crazy and having a breakdown but I'm not. I know it's hard to believe but think about it?! How could I get this dirty lying in bed?" Matt holds out his phone to show us the selfie he took when he was in bed covered in dirt. We all nod and Matt continues his story.

"As I told you before, there is a shadow cast on the hallway wall from the moonlight coming in from the bathroom window that's in the shape of a door. In this shadow, I saw a hand wave to me, motioning for me to enter the shadow. Yesterday, I decided to try to follow this man into the shadow. I knew it was a crazy idea and seriously thought I wouldn't be able to as the wall would be solid and that would be that. However, when I touched the shadow, it wasn't solid. I was able to enter it. I followed him in. It was dark but he cast a light from his body so I followed behind him for quite a while. Eventually, we fell through a shaft of some kind and landed in a pile of dirt surrounded by trees. I tried to talk to him but he didn't answer my questions. He seemed to expect me to ask different questions or to know what he wants. He was very frustrated and disappointed that I couldn't help him. I know that he needs help. It was very scary in some ways but nothing bad actually happened to me."

Mom and Derek both start to speak but Matt continues before they can. "I think he won't stop appearing in the hallway until I can find a way to help him.' Matt looks at us each individually and then finishes by saying, "I know that is very hard to believe this actually happened, but it did! Please, PLEASE believe me. I want to get this resolved and I need you to help me figure out how. When I woke up, I tried very hard to remember all the details and I wrote out these notes." He holds up this phone so we can all see he has taken detailed notes.

The room is silent for several minutes. Then mom stands up and says, "Elaine offered to feed us lunch. Let's take her up on that and then continue the conversation." Everyone but Matt stands up and moves about the room. I see mom texting Elaine and watch as she then goes over and sits down to talk with Matt. I can tell she is trying to assess his mental state. After she speaks to him for a few minutes, she goes over to chat with Brenda. After a short conversation, she heads over to Elaine's house.

Matt looks exhausted and motions for me to come over to him. He speaks softly to me and I nod, then he slowly stands up and says for everyone to hear, "I'm going back to bed now. I gave CJ my phone so you can look at my notes if you want." Brenda starts to ask him something but Matt anticipates her question. "I can't eat right now, I'm too tired." No one tries to discourage him. I walk with him to his room and make sure he's comfortable, then close his door.

When I re-enter the living room, Derek motions for us all to go out to the backyard. It is a warm day for late March and we sit at the patio table with more coffee and collect our thoughts. I start out first and say, "I think it would be good to convince Matt to get checked out at the hospital. He looks awful and I still think he is imagining all this." I glance at Brenda and notice she looks older than she did earlier in the day. She's looking at Derek to find out his opinion about Matt.

Derek stands up and begins pacing, then turns to look at us both. "I'm no expert but I think Matt is telling the truth. I don't know how it can be possible, but I just don't see any evidence anywhere around the house where Matt might have gotten so filthy. His bike doesn't have any dirt on its tracks, there are no car tracks with dirt anywhere near this house or in the garage. I checked his back pack, it's clean too." He states emphatically, *"There is no evidence to indicate that he's imagined all this."*

Before Brenda or I can respond, Elaine and mom show up carrying a tray full of a variety of sandwiches, bags of chips, and cookies. After they set the tray down, they leave again and return with paper plates, a pitcher of ice water and glasses. Elaine decides she will stay for lunch and as we are all about to sit down, we hear Kitty meowing softy. She rubs up against Derek's leg, startling him. He picks up the kitten and says, "What the heck?!?" We all turn to look and notice the normally gray kitten is now brown, the color of dirt and she is very weak.

Brenda says, "Poor Kitty, she looks as bad as Matt did in his selfie." As she says this, we all look at each other startled.

Elaine turns to me and asks, "Where's Kitty's water dish?" I run to get it. When I come back, Elaine is sitting on the ground holding Kitty and is using a napkin to wipe some of the dirt off her face. I put the water dish next to Kitty and she takes a long drink. Elaine hurries to the bathroom and returns with a towel. She wraps it around the shaking kitten, places her on a patio chair and sits down next to her. She curls up into a tight ball, closes her eyes and is soon asleep.

As we eat lunch, we talk about if it's possible that a five-month-old cat could have followed Matt into the shadow. Again, we speculate if Matt really was able to go INTO a shadow in the first place. Derek reiterates that he didn't find any evidence that Matt got himself dirty as he searched for this when he first arrived at the house. We kick around the idea if someone, somehow managed to drug Matt, give him a suggestion or idea of this man in the shadow story and then cover him with dirt. Could this same awful person cover a kitten with dirt too? I tell the group, "I don't know anyone that would do that to Matt or Kitty, what would be the motivation?" This is followed by silence.

Elaine is looking rather pale from all that she's heard over lunch. She stands up and at first, no one pays any attention to her. After a couple of minutes though, we all see she's waiting for us to acknowledge her. We all stop talking and turn to face her. Now that she has our attention, she sits back down.

"About a year after Leah had the first stoke, she told me there was a man in the hallway shadow that beckoned to her. I thought it was the side effects from the strokes or her medication. I could tell she was upset that I didn't take her seriously but she didn't press the issue. About a month later, she called me in the middle of the night saying she wasn't feeling well. I came and sat with her trying to convince her to let me take her to the emergency room. But she insisted I just sit with her and then, about 4 am, she asked me to get her medicine from the bathroom for her."

"When I entered the bathroom, the full moon was shining through the window but I didn't think anything of it. When I turned to leave, I saw the shadow on the hallway wall and a man inside motioning to me. I screamed and Leah came quickly to me. She put her arm around me and we walked past the shadow together. She then admitted that she tricked me, that she was feeling fine but wanted to find out if the Shadow Man was real. She was worried she was losing her mind. While I didn't like her deception, I understood her concern. We never spoke about it again, I guess we didn't know what to say." Elaine looks down at her hands.

Brenda says with a sharp edge to her voice, "Why didn't you call and tell me about this?"

"Ha, you would have thought we BOTH had gone off our rockers, just like you all first thought about Matt!" Elaine stands back up and starts gathering the trash and dishes from the table in a huff. Then she adds, "No one told ME what happened to Matt, you just asked me to come sit with him, which I was happy to do!" She tosses the trash back down on the table and turns away from everyone and sobs into a napkin.

Brenda walks over to Elaine and says, "Oh, Elaine, I'm sorry, I should have told you what was going on. I was so thoughtless." She holds out her arms and Elaine accepts her hug. There is now an awkward silence to say the least.

Full Moon Shadow

Derek stands and picks up the sleeping Kitty and signals for me to come with him. We knock softly on Matt's door and, getting no answer, we enter quietly. Matt's sound asleep so Derek puts Kitty next to Matt and then looks at Matt for a few minutes.

We find the others have now relocated to the living room and agree it's time to review Matt's notes from when he was in the shadow. I take Matt's phone and read aloud:

- IT IS DARK INSIDE BUT HE IS LIGHT
- TRY TO TURN BACK BUT HE GRABS ME
- I GET TRAPPED IN HIS LIGHT
- WE BOTH FALL INTO A SHAFT
- LAND HARD ON SOFT DIRT
- STILL DARK AND HE IS BRIGHTER THAN BEFORE
- HE IS TOO BRIGHT AND TOO HOT
- I CLOSE MY EYES AND LOSE CONSCIOUSNESS
- WAKE UP, SEE TALL TREES ALL AROUND
- SHADOW MAN IS NO LONGER BRIGHT, NOW HE'S MUTED TANS & GRAYS
- I TELL HIM MY NAME, ASK HIM HIS NAME AND WHERE ARE WE?
- HE REPLIES "MY NAME IS LEON HOKE; THIS IS MY HOME"
- TELLS ME I ASK THE WRONG QUESTIONS, I'M NO HELP TO HIM
- I FEEL INTENSE ANGER FROM HIM
- HE PUTS HIS ARMS OVERHEAD AND TURNS INTO LIGHT AGAIN AND DISAPPEARS
- THERE IS A THUNDERSTORM BUT NO RAIN
- I CROUCH IN THE CLEARING
- THEN I'M HOME ON THE BATHROOM FLOOR
- I TRY TO STAND UP BUT FAINT
- WAKE UP IN BED AND AM CONFUSED, I DON'T REMEMBER WHAT HAPPENED

Full Moon Shadow

I ask Elaine, "When did Leah she first notice the man in the shadow?" She thinks about it for a couple of minutes.

"I'm not sure exactly but I'll try to remember." Elaine looks at me concerned. "Do you think that's important?" I shrug my shoulders.

We talk for a long time about what we might do to help Matt. We wish we had "proof" that Matt and possibly Kitty were actually inside the shadow. Since Elaine had cleaned up the dirt from the floor, we can't look for footprints. The bathroom window shows no signs of being tampered with and is not dirty at all. Suddenly I get an idea and stand up.

I leave the room to go get the box of the microfiber cloths Matt uses to dust the furniture and go into the hallway. Derek follows me. "I see where you're going with this and I like it! But wait, I want to grab something from the garage." He comes back with painter's tape and his cell phone. Now everyone is gathering to watch. I take the white wipe and use it to dust the beige painted wall where the shadow appears. I turn it over and look at it; there is brown dirt on the rag, the same color of the dirt that was on Matt and Kitty.

Derek says "Let's check the hallway wall where the shadow DOESN'T appear." He picks up a new wipe and swipes further down the hall. He turns it over and it is clean. Everyone gasps. Derek and I use painter's tape to document where there is dirt versus not. After we finish, we see the pieces of tape around the dusty section of the wall have formed a shape that a short man would fit through, aka Matt. We all exhale our collective breaths. Finally, tangible proof it really happened.

We now turn our thoughts to the immediate needs to help Matt. We come up with a plan, mostly formulated by Matt's parents. Derek summarizes for us all: "Sally was able to break CJ's dorm contract so he needs to be out of the dorms ASAP. That means CJ will be able to move in with Matt tomorrow." He breaks from his summary and turns to me to ask, "CJ, what furniture do you want replaced to make Leah's office into your bedroom?"

Full Moon Shadow

"The only thing I'd like new is a bed and a study table. I like that old heavy bookcase. Eventually, I would like to get a new computer chair but can use Leah's old one for now." Derek and mom nod in agreement. "Tonight, I will sleep in the dorm. That way, I can get my things all packed and ready to move in here tomorrow. I take it you two will stay on the hide-a-bed tonight?" Brenda and Derek nod in agreement. I turn to mom and ask, "Where are you sleeping?

"On the living room couch and will stay in Davis to get you settled. Also, I want to be here when we ask Matt more questions about what happened in the shadow."

Derek resumes his summary, "Sally, I'm assuming you will order a new bed and mattress for CJ?" She nods her head. "Brenda, you will shop locally for a study table for CJ's room. CJ, I'm very glad you like the bookshelf as it's too heavy to easily move. Sally and Brenda already agreed they will clean out Leah's desk and then we will move it to the garage to make room for the study table. I will move the boxes into the garage tonight or first thing tomorrow."

Derek looks at me and repeats what he said earlier today. "CJ, are you sure you are willing to stay here with Matt *every night* until this issue is resolved?" Derek sounds like a parent leaving their child for the first time with a sitter.

Brenda pipes up and says "Really Derek, I think it most important on nights there might be a full moon, don't you agree? CJ doesn't need to babysit Matt every night." She smiles at CJ and then at Derek.

"No, that's for sure, I don't need a sitter *EVERY* night." We all look up at a smiling Matt standing there holding a very sleepy, dirty Kitty. "When's dinner? I'm starving."

Full Moon Shadow

Matt

Everyone in the living room looks up surprised to see me. After their initial shock at hearing my voice, they look relieved to see me awake and alert.

"Matt, I'm so happy to see you looking refreshed!" Mom rushes over to hug me and is beaming.

"Dude, we've got so much to tell you." CJ says from the recliner with his mom sitting next to him. They both are smiling at me. Dad comes over to me with a more somber look and gives me a hug which he doesn't do that often.

"We believe you now son, we believe you." He sounds a bit rough and when he finally lets me go, I see his eyes are moist. Mom urges me to sit on the couch and then she and dad sit next to me. I put Kitty on the couch next to me.

Sally tells me, "There are sandwiches leftover from lunch, I will bring you a plate. What would you like to drink?"

"A glass of milk. Thanks Sally." She heads into the kitchen and comes back in a few minutes with a plate in one hand and a large glass of milk in the other. When dad sees this, he gets up and sets a TV tray in front of me and then sits back down. Kitty crawls into dad's lap and curls up.

Everyone tries to just let me eat but they can't contain their enthusiasm. CJ gets to his feet and paces the room while he summarizes what I missed while I was asleep. It is interesting to hear that both Aunt Leah and Elaine saw the man in the shadow several months ago. My parents don't want me to stay in the house alone and have asked CJ to move in with me. I am relieved to know I won't be here by myself. It is weird though, that he's moving in without me asking him myself. Before I can think about it more, CJ continues. He tells me that they found dust particles within the hallway shadow area that match my shape. He says they feel this provides evidence that I really did come out of the wall covered in dirt. When he says this, there is a long pause.

73

Full Moon Shadow

"Honestly, I don't care that you needed proof, I'm just relieved you all now believe me. I was worried I might wake up in a strait jacket." After my statement, no one makes eye contact with me which makes me realize my concern wasn't unreasonable. I break the uncomfortable silence by asking, "I wonder if Kitty got that dirty from sleeping next to me?"

Elaine says, "Kitty showed up when we sat down to eat lunch. She was weak, thirsty, and covered in dirt. We think she must have followed you into the shadow." Hearing this, I reach over and pat Kitty gently even though she's sound asleep on dad's lap.

Elaine stands to go. "It's been a long day and I'm going to head home." Mom and dad stand too and thank Elaine for all she's done. When they come back into the living room and sit back down, the mood has shifted.

"Matt, we need to ask you more questions about what happened when you went into the shadow. We also have more questions about the two other times you saw the hand waving in the shadow, during the January and February full moons." Dad looks at me a bit worried.

I nod my head as I was expecting this. After I finish my milk, I begin. "At the first event, when I saw a hand waving at me, I didn't know what was going on. I didn't take it seriously as I thought it was a prank. In the dorms, practical jokes are common."

"But you saw something, what exactly did you see?" Mom says.

Thinking hard, I dredge up the memory. "First, I saw a hand on the doorframe of the shadow. Later, I saw a hand waving at me as if to say, 'Come on in.'

"Was the hand on the inside or outside of the door frame?" Dad looks worried.

I shiver thinking about what he's implying; maybe the Shadow Man was INSIDE the house and just returning into the shadow. "His palm was flat against the inside of the doorframe; I only saw the outline of his fingers."

Full Moon Shadow

Dad says, "Okay please go over the second full moon incident, the one about the rain in your bedroom."

"It kind of makes sense that I would have a nightmare about rain given what a day it had been. There was a huge wind and rain storm that day that blew over trees, flooded roads, and damaged property throughout Davis and the region. I helped some neighbors clean up afterwards and then had trouble getting to sleep that night." No one interjects so I continue.

"In my dream, it was raining in my bedroom so it made sense to me to go get my rain gear from the bathroom which I had left hanging over the shower rod. However, when I got to the bathroom, it wasn't raining there. I dried off with a towel and started to go back to bed but I see the full moon shadow with the man waving for me to follow him. I see it is still raining in my bedroom, so I think, 'Why not?' Slowly, I entered the shadow. It was very dark and warm inside it which surprised me. Suddenly, I felt the Shadow Man grab my forearm and it felt like it was burning me. That's when I woke up and felt very cold except for my arm where he grabbed me.

"What did you do when you woke up?" CJ asks.

"I got out of bed and went into the bathroom to look at the moon and for the man in the shadow. He wasn't there. I touched the door frame of the shadow, it felt warm and when I let go, I felt very cold and dizzy so decided to go back to bed. But my arm still hurt so I looked at it for indications that it had been burned but found nothing. Eventually, I was able to fall back to sleep."

"The next morning, I woke up with a fever and sick to my stomach so it made sense at the time that it was just a bad dream. I was sick all day so it was easy to convince myself it wasn't real. But now, after what happened last night, maybe in part it WAS real." I feel frustrated about not knowing if it was a nightmare or real and can't make eye contact with anyone.

Dad says "Let's take a break." He moves the TV tray and takes my empty dishes into the kitchen and comes back with a tray of

Full Moon Shadow

beverages for us all. We all choose our drinks and then sit back down. I take a few sips of my drink and look up at them warily.

Dad asks, "Are you ready for the last review?"

"Didn't the notes I wrote give you enough detail?" I say this a bit more sharply than I intended but at least they know I want to get this over with.

Sally says gently, "The notes helped but we still have some questions. We will try to be brief but remember, we are doing this because we are trying to figure out what we can do to help you." She pauses and then continues. "In your nightmare, you decided to follow the Shadow Man because it was raining in your bedroom. But this time, you are awake and you consciously decide to follow him. This makes me think the nightmare might have been more of a warm up created by the Shadow Man to get you ready for the real thing. What do you think?"

"I HAVE NO FREAKING IDEA!" I am embarrassed that I exploded like that at Sally. I'm surprised that no one reacts to my outburst; they continue as if nothing happened.

Dad asks "Do you have any idea where this place with the dirt and trees might be? I mean, does it remind you of a real place?"

Thinking about this, I nod slowly. "It seems like it might be somewhere not far from here. There are a few wooded areas where I have gone for hikes that kind of remind me of the place in the shadow." Dad nods.

Sally says "I have several questions that I will just say all together: Are you sure he said his name is Leon Hoke? You said he was sitting on a fallen tree. Any idea what kind of tree? Last question, I promise, the dirt area you landed in, how big of an area was it?"

"His voice was hoarse and hard to understand at first but I thought he said his name was Leon Hoke. I have no idea what kind of tree he was sitting on, it was too dark to make it out, even with the full moon. The dirt area, hmm, it was a round area, maybe six to eight feet across." Sally nods. I look at mom and CJ to see what they want to ask me.

Full Moon Shadow

Mom asks, "You said you fainted in the bathroom but woke up later in your bed. Do you have any idea how you got from the bathroom to your bedroom?"

I shake my head no and add, "Sorry, no idea."

"CJ, do you have any questions for me?"

"Yes, I do. You told us Leon Hoke didn't like the questions you asked. Have you thought of what questions he wanted you to ask? Or what you wish you had asked instead?"

"Yes, I want to find out three things: 1) What he needs from me, 2) Why he thinks I can help him, and 3) How does he think I can help him." They are all nodding at this. Everyone puts down their notes which I take it to mean we are done. I get up and excuse myself and go to the bathroom. I'm relieved the inquisition is over. I stay there for quite a while staring out the window and looking at the moon. As I exit, I look at the hallway for a long time before joining the others.

In my absence, I find out they ordered pizza for dinner. I get up to go find Kitty and pick her up. I whisper to her, "What do you want to know, Kitty?"

As we eat pizza, dad goes over the list of who's doing what to get ready for CJ moving in. He finishes his list and says, "It's almost dark and I was hoping to move the boxes into the garage tonight."

Alarm bells go off in my head at this announcement. "Wait, what is happening to the boxes?" Dad explains how they are trying to clear out as much of Aunt Leah's office as they can to make it a bedroom for CJ by tomorrow. That means the boxes and the desk will be moved to the garage.

"I need to tell you something first." They all look at me startled and kind of worried. "It's not about the moon shadow, nothing like that. It's just…. hold on, let me go get it and I will explain." I rush into Aunt Leah's office, get the packet from the desk drawer and bring it to the living room. I pull out the letter and notebook and explain. "Aunt Leah left this for me. Dad gave it to me after

Full Moon Shadow

his birthday party." I read the letter aloud and then pass it around.

Mom says, "Dad's birthday was March 2, why are you just looking for this object now?" She sounds annoyed I didn't read the letter as soon as I received it.

I feel myself getting flustered as I attempt to explain. "I opened the package from Aunt Leah a couple of weeks ago but decided to wait until finals were over before starting on the quest to find the missing object. After finals, I looked in the yard with no luck. I can't remember where I used to dig in the yard for 'treasure.' I was going to look through the boxes in the office yesterday to find the one with my name on it but, as you know, that didn't happen." I let that hang in the air as they know what happened yesterday.

Mom looks a bit sorry to have spoken out. But then says in the tone she did when I was a young child, "Oh well, I'm sure it really isn't anything important." I feel myself getting agitated all over again especially when she adds, "You know Aunt Leah could be a bit eccentric."

"Okay, maybe it's nothing like you say. However, it was HER LETTER TO ME and I plan to continue to look!" Dad is nodding his head while mom still looks skeptical. CJ and Sally just are watching this conversation like it is a tennis match, going back and forth between mom and me at opposite ends of the couch. I look directly at mom and tell her, "Please, any yard repair receipts that you find in her desk, save them for me to review." I turn and say, "Dad, can you please look carefully at the boxes and set aside any marked with my name?"

Before dad can answer, CJ says, "I will look at each box for your name, I promise bro. When I find the box, I will put it in your room, okay?" I nod at this appreciatively and then look back towards mom.

"Well, we don't have a lot of time to go through each and every item in the desk...." Mom looks at dad for support. He just stares at her with an expression I can't read. He seems to be holding his breath.

Sally turns to me and says, "I will be helping with the sorting and can look specifically for yard receipts." She turns to mom and gives her a tentative smile.

Mom hesitates and then says, "Okay Matt, we will do as you ask." Dad lets out a breath. I feel relief flood over me.

CJ says quietly, "Let's go outside for a bit." He can feel the tension in the room too. As we go outside through the front door, we see Elaine on her front porch and walk over to her.

"Elaine, do you think I could give Kitty a bath when she's more awake?"

"It might be possible. Some cats don't mind baths. It's important that the water isn't too hot or cold. Do you want me to help you?"

"That would be great, thanks! Maybe tomorrow?"

She nods her head and asks, "Is everything alright?" She must sense there is some reason we aren't inside with the others.

CJ explains. "It is a little tense in there right now." He looks at me silently asking that I explain.

I tell her about the letter Aunt Leah left for me and how I have been looking for this unknown object. I reluctantly add, "Mom is resisting doing whatever she can to help me find it."

Elaine doesn't seem at all surprised. "Matt, family dynamics are complicated. Your mom was very sad when her mom died and that you wouldn't have a grandmother. Yet, when you and Leah became close, your mom was a bit jealous. Think about it; you loved coming to see Leah, didn't you. Did you also spend lots of quality time with your mom?" When I don't reply, she asks, "What do you have in common with your mom?"

That is a great question and I stop to think. "She's a neat freak and so am I. We both have sweet tooths, especially chocolate..."

Full Moon Shadow

I try to think of other things but I'm stumped. "Okay, I can see she might be a bit jealous." I am a bit embarrassed.

CJ says, "What does that have to do with why Brenda doesn't want to help Matt find this object? I would think she would be as curious about it as we are." He looks to Elaine hoping for a good answer.

She replies, "Give her time." CJ and I both nod our heads at this and then Elaine asks, "Do you want help finding the item Leah misplaced? I can come over 10 am tomorrow morning, help bathe Kitty and then read her letter. Maybe I can come up with some ideas of where to look."

I agree and then CJ and I start our walk around the block to have a talk.

Full Moon Shadow

CJ

After our conversation with Elaine, Matt is pretty quiet as we start out walking. After a few minutes of silence between us though, I stop and turn to him. "Dude, I need to ask you something." He looks up at me with interest. "I've been wanting to ask you for a long time if I could move in with you. Now, because of what happened, your parents want me to do just that. But I need to know if YOU want me to move in?"

Matt is slow to answer and doesn't make eye contact with me as he says, "CJ, I was thinking about asking you to move in for the last few weeks. I have two concerns though. I want you as a housemate but not Darla." Now he looks at me and elaborates. "Now that you and Darla are back together, you might want her to stay over frequently. But I'm not ready for that. My second concern is what is going on right now in the hallway. You know?"

Now it's my turn to be embarrassed as I didn't even consider Darla as a possible concern. But I can see having a third person, especially female in the house might be awkward. Plus, we're dealing with our uninvited guest, Shadow Man. "Whoa, I understand completely."

Matt looks relieved and adds, "I want to get rid of the shadow dude first and then we can figure out the other details, okay?" I smile at this and offer my hand. After we shake, we walk in comfortable silence before heading back to the house.

Once inside, we notice the tension has eased. Brenda and Derek are sitting next to each other looking at an old photo album they found in Leah's office. Matt goes in search of Kitty. I tell them about seeing Elaine outside and that she's coming in the morning to help bathe Kitty. They nod and give me a quick smile before turning their attention back to the photos.

I also tell mom about Elaine and her theory about why Brenda was so bent out of shape. Mom finds this theory interesting. "I was wondering why Brenda was being so difficult about helping Matt with Leah's request!" She looks relieved at the simple explanation. "Hopefully, she can help." I agree with her and let her get back to sorting through files.

Before I go to my dorm for the night, I help Derek move the boxes to the garage. I find not one, but three boxes with Matt's name and put them in his room. Matt is extremely happy and he starts to go through the boxes immediately. He barely waves goodbye when I say I'm heading to the dorm. I'm glad he has something else to focus on to get his mind off the shadow person and what might happen next.

Full Moon Shadow

Matt

I heard CJ say goodnight but was focused on sorting through the three boxes he found with my name. Two boxes have documents, drawings, and photos related to me that Aunt Leah kept. Most of this, I'm tossing out but it is nice to see what she saved over the years. There are newspaper articles with photos of my high school debate team getting an award, cards and letters I sent to her (at my mom's encouragement) for special occasions, and various drawings and paintings I made for her when I was in grade school. I set these two boxes aside to go through in more detail later.

In the third box, there is bubble wrap cushioning three cans of my 'backyard treasures.' The containers are actually old Christmas cans which are typically used to put cookies and other treats for holiday gifts. I spread out an old towel on my study table to prevent things from rolling off and I start going through the first can and sort what I find into piles. I don't see much of what I would think is worthy of keeping. There are lots of small rocks, pieces of shells, tiny sticks and string like moss. I see a few intact items, mostly shells and non-descript rocks but nothing of value that I can tell.

I stand up and stretch and notice that I still need to make the bed. Sighing, I carry the dirty bedding to the garage to start the laundry. When I open the door to the garage, I'm startled as mom, dad and Sally are all in the garage. They stop talking when they see me. Mom says, "We were trying to be quiet as we thought you might be asleep." She notices what I'm carrying and says, "Oh honey, let me do that for you."

"Thanks, mom. I can use a sleeping bag for tonight since my bedding is dirty but thought I should get these in the wash tonight."

"Beat you to it dear. When we went to make up the hide-a-bed, we realized there were no spare sheets so we went to Target." She opens the dryer and pulls out brand-new sheets that have just been washed. She then turns around and shows me a still wrapped navy-blue blanket labeled, Queen Sized Comforter. We swap the bedding between us and I turn to go back inside.

I must have looked tired or something as Sally stops me by placing her hand on my arm. I turn to see what she wants. She looks me in the eyes and says, "Matt, it will be okay." I feel myself flush with annoyance. How does she know what will happen? She really has no idea! Somehow though, I manage to control my emotions as I know she means well.

Without meeting her gaze, I manage to say, "Thanks."

*   *   *

I'm kind of nervous about giving Kitty a bath thinking it will be a fight to get her in the water. It turns out, Kitty doesn't mind the bath until the water gets too cold. When she starts to try to jump out of the bathroom sink, I hand her to Elaine who is ready with a towel to wrap up the dripping wet cat. She takes her to the living room to finish drying her and comb out he fur. I stay behind to clean the sink; it takes a while as there is dirt and cat hair on the counter and floor too.

When I finally join Elaine and Kitty in the living room, I see that Kitty looks a lot better but she's now washing herself as only cats do. Smiling, I go get Aunt Leah's letter and give it to Elaine to read. She takes it to the dining room table saying, "The light is better in here. Can I look at her journal too?" I nod and bring it to her. She thumbs through it impatiently. "She stopped entering in the journal about the same time she had her first fall. See here?"

I look at the journal and see the last entry was in 2021. "I'm thinking of making a list of the yard work receipts. Do you think I should just focus on the last couple of years?"

"That would be the most logical. After all, that is when her memory started to slip. Too bad we didn't know she was having mini strokes until later." She pauses in thought. "You might want to ask Stan about the yard work he did for her. He never would take any money from her so there wouldn't be any receipts. He lives on the other side of me."

Full Moon Shadow

"He's the one that had the tree fall on his car, right?"

"That's correct."

"Okay, I'll talk to Stan. Do you have any ideas of what she might have found or where she might have put it?"

Elaine shakes her head. "She and I told each other everything, or so I thought. But after I saw the man in the shadow waving at me, we both shied away from talking about difficult subjects." I can tell she's still thinking about my question though. "Anything really important to her, she put on the bookcase or in the desk in her office. Have you looked there?"

"I looked on the bookcase the night before I went into the shadow but didn't search her desk. Mom and Sally are now sorting through her desk drawers and files. If they find anything out of the ordinary, I'm sure they'll let me know. Last night, I started sorting through the boxes she left me and the cans of treasures I found in the back yard. Maybe she put the object into one of the two boxes that I haven't finished sorting yet."

We both read over Aunt Leah's letter once again. I ask Elaine, "I can't remember where I used to dig in her back yard. Do you happen to know?" I look hopefully at Elaine.

She shakes her head no but then looks optimistic and says, "Let's go into the back yard, maybe it will remind me of something." We go outside and look around together. "Sorry Matt, nothing is standing out that might help you. Once you go through all the receipts, let's talk again. Maybe that will help." Elaine pats me on the shoulder and heads home.

The rest of the day is busy with all the activity at the house. I heard Sally on the phone ordering a bed for CJ. After her call, she leaves to go to the dorm to help CJ move his things here to the house. Mom finishes sorting the desk and hands me a large envelope of yard receipts to go through. I thank her and give her a brief hug and take the receipts to my room. Then I help dad move the desk to the garage. Mom orders a new study table for

Full Moon Shadow

CJ to be delivered today and then goes to a second-hand store and buys a night stand and dresser for him.

*   *   *

Later that day, we all help CJ unload his things and now the room looks more like CJ's room than Aunt Leah's office. The study table is covered with his books, his backpack is propping open the closet door, and his clothes are strewn over the dresser and the hide-a-bed. The only things left of Aunt Leah's are the antique book case and her desk chair, both are covered with CJ's jacket and dorm room stuff. After looking at all of this, I can't help but grin. Just then, I hear mom calling us for dinner.

"This soup was delicious, Brenda." Mom smiles at the complement as she knows Sally is a foodie and a very good cook. Sally adds, "Since I have the whole week off, I'm staying one more night with the guys. That is, if they don't mind?" She gets up and starts to clear the table.

"Of course, you're welcome to stay another night, Sally." I am wondering though, why she wants to spend another night on the lumpy couch. I ask my parents, "What time are you heading home?"

"We are leaving about 7 pm hoping the traffic has lessened by then. I think things are okay here now that CJ is living with you."

"Yes dad, that's all good. But we still haven't talked about what the plan is to deal with the man in the shadow problem." I look around at the table and no one says anything.

CJ says, "I've been doing some research on some of the things you talked about in your notes and what you told us. So far, I haven't found anything helpful."

Sally says something but I can't make out what she says. Before I can ask her to repeat, dad jumps in and says "We still have a few weeks before the next full moon. We're hoping to get a more definite plan before then."

Full Moon Shadow

Now mom looks at dad and stands up. "In the meantime, Derek, please show us what you did to keep the shadow from appearing?" We all get up from the table and look into the bathroom. The window used to have flowery curtains that I took down when I first moved in. I meant to replace them but never got around to it. There are now very dark curtains hanging over the window which completely blocks the light from outside. CJ, Sally and mom are delighted at this and turn to me to see my reaction.

I hesitate before expressing an unenthusiastic, "Thanks." I can see in their faces they are all surprised at my lack of enthusiasm. "Sorry, I just think that is not the solution but a delay tactic. Leon Hoke is still going to be waiting for someone to help him." No one has a reply to that.

After we finish cleaning up from dinner, I help my parents load their stuff into the car and give them hugs goodbye. "Thanks for coming when I called you." They chat for a bit more with CJ and Sally and then drive away.

While CJ and Sally go for a walk, I get out the yard work receipts and Aunt Leah's gardening journal. I start to draft a summary of the receipts and create a sketch of her back yard to help me get a handle on what was done over the years. I still need to talk to Stan to find out what yard work he did for Aunt Leah. I check the time; it's is only 7:30 pm so I go over to see if he's home. Lucky for me, he's home and invites me to come in.

As he's thanking me once again for helping with the clean up after the big wind storm, his wife, Cara joins us carrying a tray with plate of fresh-out-of-the-oven chocolate chip cookies and glasses of milk. (I'm in heaven!) We make small talk while I devour the cookies before I explain why I came over. "Aunt Leah left me a mystery to solve. She found something in her yard that she then misplaced. In case you hadn't heard, in the last couple of years of her life, she'd been having mini strokes which affected her memory."

Full Moon Shadow

Cara replies, "Yes, we noticed her memory loss and talked to Elaine about it. It was sad, very sad. We miss her greatly." She then looks at Stan who nods his head at her ever so slightly. Cara turns back to me and adds, "We were surprised there wasn't a service for her." She looks at me questioningly.

I didn't expect this and it takes me a while to know what to say. "Mom and dad have her ashes and have discussed having something for her but they never settled on anything. I will ask them what they've decided and we will let you know."

"Thanks Matt, we know it's hard for families to know what to do. If you don't mind a suggestion, a Celebration of Life party somewhere here in Davis would be nice. Leah always liked a good party." Stan smiles as he says this.

"Okay, thanks for the suggestion." They nod and I take a deep breath, ready to change the subject back to why I stopped by. "As I mentioned, Aunt Leah found something in her yard that she thought was important and put it somewhere to deal with later. Then, with her memory loss, she couldn't remember where she put it. I've looked and can't find anything that seems important. I've talked to Elaine about this and she thinks it might have been sometime after she had that huge oak tree removed from her back yard. She mentioned you did some yard work for her related to that tree. If you can recall the specifics of the work you did for her around that time, that might help me with this mystery."

I'm surprised they don't ask for more details but instead, Stan gets up and comes back with his cell phone. Turns out, he has a very detailed calendar on his phone and even better memory. I go home smiling with more information to add to my backyard map and notes.

Later that evening, Sally, CJ and I are relaxing in the living room each looking at our phones. Sally breaks the silence by announcing, "Matt, I think you might want to try meditation or maybe even hypnosis to help you with your memories." I'm shocked by this suggestion. I glance at CJ and he shrugs his shoulders as if to say, 'Why not give it a try?'

Full Moon Shadow

Sally continues, "We need to better understand everything that happened in order to try to help you with the Shadow Man. Some of your missing memories might be important. Or the memories might help you find the missing object Leah misplaced." I unenthusiastically nod my head. "Tomorrow morning, I will go over some meditation techniques and help you get started. Is that okay with you?" Again, I nod my head in agreement and I try my best not to roll my eyes. Now I know why she wanted to stay another night. I excuse myself and head to bed.

*   *   *

The next morning, Sally and I sit in the living room to discuss meditation while CJ does the breakfast dishes. I politely listen to Sally tell me about the benefits of relaxation then listen to the YouTube meditation she has suggested. I'm pleasantly surprised it isn't too sappy and tell her that I think it sounds promising. I'm thinking it may help me fall asleep more quickly. She also talks about using hypnosis to help me remember things like where I used to dig in the backyard and other things I can't remember. When she starts going into detail though, she can tell I'm not interested and stops mid-sentence. "Okay, Matt, I get it. Enough for now. But really, contact me if you want to try it."

Sally gets up and starts to gather her things. Her friend, Rita, will be arriving shortly to give her a ride home. "Thanks for everything, Sally. It meant a lot that you came to help me." I give her a heartfelt hug goodbye. She seems grateful to hear my appreciation and hugs me back. CJ walks out to the car with her and once he comes back in the house, we smile at each other like nerds. We are officially college roommates once again!

CJ and I have another reason to be happy as today is March 28, the official first day of spring quarter. Even though the first day of classes isn't until April 1, the few days in-between allow students time to get settled back into school mode, adjust their schedules, purchase supplies, reconnect with friends, and things like that. CJ and I talk a bit about the upcoming quarter before we both retreat to our rooms to start the process. I feel a collective buzz in the air all around me as I know fellow UC Davis students throughout Davis are doing the same. It doesn't take me that long to do what I need to do and am about to head to the kitchen to see what I can eat for lunch, when I hear CJ's phone ring from his bedroom.

"Hello, Darla? You're back. Did you have a good trip?" He is excited and talking so loudly, I can hear every word from down the hallway. He must be listening for a long while as I don't hear him speak again for quite a while. "How about I meet you downtown?" I note a long pause and then, "Yeah, that's fine, see you in about 30 minutes!" He comes bursting out of his room and into my room. "Matt, I'm thinking of going to meet Darla downtown for lunch. I'll be back by 5 pm." I notice he is stating this but kind of asking for my okay at the same time. I can't help but smile at his checking in with me even though I heard him tell her he would be there in 30 minutes.

"Sure, that's fine. Tell her I said hi. I'm going for a bike ride after I grab some lunch." I start toward the kitchen.

"Great! Oh, Matt? I was wondering if you heard back from Kim?"

"Yeah, she's back with Simon, but that's fine." He gives me a shrug and then waves as he heads to the garage for his bike.

I think I'll make a grocery list after I fix my sandwich but when I open the fridge door, I find it's stocked full of food. Must be mom's doing. After I eat, I make sure Kitty's in the house and I give her a pat on the head before going to the garage for my bike. When I enter the garage, I notice it's been swept, the washer and dryer wiped down, and the cobwebs removed from the corners and shelves. Mom's doing again. As I look around at the tidy garage, I think about her. I realize that she can't help being who she is. Sure, she can be tactless at times which is embarrassing. When I think about it, maybe that is where I got my short fuse from. I mean, look at her chosen profession, she's an accountant. I can't help but smile at that.

Full Moon Shadow

It makes sense what Elaine said about mom being jealous of Aunt Leah. I wasn't that interested in the places mom suggested we go, like museums and shows. Instead, I wanted to go for hikes with my dad, visit Aunt Leah to help her in the garden or go on nature walks. I'll try to be more aware of that from now on.

I decide to ride out to the west side of campus where there's a nature trail along Putah Creek with a lot of native trees and plants. Aunt Leah and I used to ride our bikes to this same nature trail when I was in middle school. Sometimes we would swim in the creek in the late spring. There's a rope swing people use to jump into the cool water. Of course, when I would swing out, it was with a Tarzan yell. She laughed at my antics.

Once I reach the entrance to the trail, I don't see anyone at the parking lot or on the trail. I feel a bit uncertain about walking very far by myself. I know this is an irrational feeling on my part. The whole going-into-the-shadow experience has me afraid of my own shadow. Ironic, huh? I hope this situation with the Shadow Man will be over with soon.

I walk a short distance along the trail and hesitate to go much further so I sit down on a bench that overlooks the creek. As I look at the fast-flowing water from all the recent storms, I think about the last couple of days. Edward texted me the day after we went to the movies to give me details for the next hike but I never responded. I'm sure he's wondering why I didn't get back to him. I'm not likely to say, "On the night of the full moon, I followed a stranger into a shadow." I can only imagine the shocked look I would get if I told him this. Hmm, maybe add, "Bra-HA-HA-HA!" in a monstrous voice. Man, my sense of humor is lame. I think of a more believable answer and text him, "Sorry I didn't get back to you. I had the flu." Soon after, I hear a ping and see a thumbs up emoji followed by TTYL.

As I'm putting my phone in my pocket, I hear someone on the trail; it's a family with their dog pulling them along. That makes me feel better about hiking a longer distance so I wait for them to pass me by and then walk along behind them. We don't get very

Full Moon Shadow

far as their dog keeps stopping to pee and sniff and I have to hold back. The dad notices me and steps aside to let me pass. I shake my head and turn back the other way to head home.

CJ is home when I get there and busy in the kitchen. "MMM! Is that chili I smell?"

He turns down the music and nods his head. "Almost ready! Darla says hi." I can tell he's in a good mood. He tells me over dinner that he got the chili recipe from his mom while he was at home.

"Thanks for cooking, this is awesome!" I must have glanced at the kitchen though as CJ gives me an embarrassed look.

'Hey, sorry about the mess. I'll clean up." He starts to get up but I jump up.

"I don't mind cleaning up. It is great to eat something I didn't make." We both laugh at this. While I'm putting away the leftovers, I see there's enough for at least a couple more meals. Smiling, I turn the music up and start to load the dishwasher.

*   *   *

On Saturday, I look at my wall calendar, I realize tomorrow is Easter Sunday, March 31. That gives me the idea to have a brunch here at the house. That is, if we can round up a few friends available to join us. CJ looks a bit surprised and asks, "Are you sure you're okay having people over?"

"Yeah, it won't be big deal as it's during the day." We find that Darla, Toni, Jed, and Edward are all available. CJ is excited to practice his cooking skills and starts to plan. He texts his mom and she suggests he keep it simple. With that in mind, brunch consists of blueberry muffins made from a mix and eggs scrambled with ham and cheese. I make coffee and toast which I mostly don't burn. Toni brings strawberries from the Davis Farmer's Market and Darla brings cookies. Jed and Edward bring nothing but their appetites.

Full Moon Shadow

Darla stays behind to help clean up after everyone else has left. She comes to talk to me after the dishes are done and says, "CJ thinks you might need some help looking through some rocks and shells." When I don't say anything, she continues, "My major is anthropology, remember?"

A light bulb is shining over my head now. I had been working on sorting through the treasures off and on these last few days. I now have four piles: black rocks, mixed colored rocks, shells, and organic material like twigs and moss. "Sorry, I'd forgotten that. Do you want to look at the stuff I saved from the back yard?"

"Most definitely, yes." I show her my piles still spread out on my study table. She spends a few minutes picking up various pieces and seems excited after a few minutes of looking. "Can I take a few of these to show my professor and take photos of the piles?" I agree and get some baggies for her to put things in. Darla puts the baggies carefully in her back pack.

I thank her for her help and walk with her to the door and say goodbye. Back in my room, I stare at the piles and wonder what she found that got her so excited. I carefully place the separated piles in large baggies and put them in my dresser drawer. If Darla hadn't looked at them so carefully, I might have just tossed them all in the trash. I'm so glad I didn't.

CHAPTER 5: APRIL, 2024

CJ

We are now almost two weeks into the spring quarter and I'm doing great. However, Matt is still struggling. When I try to talk to him, he brushes me off so I'm surprised when he asks if I have time to talk. "It was great of your mom to suggest I use meditation; it has been helping me get to sleep. I wasn't so interested when she suggested I try self-hypnosis to help me remember things." He glances at me with a guilty expression before continuing. "I thought I could remember on my own but I'm not getting anywhere. Can you give me her cell number? Or maybe you call her first?"

I nod my head in agreement. "We can call her right now." I dial and she answers on the first ring.

"CJ, I was just about to call you as there are two things I need to tell you. I goofed when I ordered your new bed and mattress; they were delivered here instead of Davis."

"That's okay mom, I understand."

"Thanks for understanding, darlin! The second thing I need to tell you is that Derek, Brenda and I have come up with a plan. We will be coming to Davis April 20, three days before the next full moon. I will bring your bed then in the truck."

"That's great news mom! I'm putting you on speaker phone now so Matt can hear too. We look forward to hearing all about the plan."

Full Moon Shadow

Sally hesitates, "We are still working out some of the specifics so it would be easier to wait. Also, we feel it would be best if we discuss this in person." I look at Matt and shrug.

Matt says, "Okay, we understand and can wait. Sally, on another subject, if you're still willing, I'd like you to teach me about self-hypnosis."

"Sure, Matt! I'd be happy to do that. How about tomorrow afternoon?" Matt agrees and is about to hang up but I hold up my hand to stop him.

"Mom, do you and Matt's parents know that Saturday, April 20 is Picnic Day here at UC Davis?"

"Yes, darling, we know. It's the campus big open house with a parade and a whole lot more. We already made motel reservations. See you then." She hangs up before I can say anything more.

Matt and I look at the now silent phone then turn to look at each other. Picnic Day is the annual open house event that UC Davis has every year. It started out as a small event over 100 years ago but now is a huge event that averages over 70,000 attendees and more than 200 activities. There's a parade, dog races, a band competition, animal displays, kiddie fair, and more. In other words, it's a madhouse with people, cars, bikes, and parties.

"Well, I kind of thought our parents might want to attend since it is a chance for them to tour the campus and see the department displays and all that. But what timing, huh?" I nod and shake my head.

Full Moon Shadow

Matt

It took me a while to get comfortable and just sit here on the swing seat in the back yard and not be distracted by my own thoughts and sounds. I'm on the phone with Sally using ear buds which is helping me focus on her voice. In a soothing voice, she speaks to me very quietly but clearly. "You are in a calm place, with no distractions, your eyes are gently closed. Take a few deep breaths and with each breath, go deeper into your peaceful place. You are walking down a long hallway, with each step, you go deeper into relaxation. Now you are in your most relaxed state and in your mind, you can remember what it was like to be here, with no worries, just you and your Aunt Leah, working in her yard. Take another deep breath and think about the warmth of the day and let your mind wander here in your aunt's beautiful back yard. That's it, slowly breathe in and out. I'm going to stop speaking while you keep your eyes closed and let your memories come to you."

I'm now hardly aware that I'm in the backyard sitting on the swing. When Sally stops talking, I only notice the gentle sounds of activity in the back yard: birds chirping and squirrels scampering. I feel peaceful, almost sleepy. I notice my breath is very even and gentle. In my mind, I see the following scene before me:

Aunt Leah is finishing planting some flowers at the edge of the patio. My younger self gets up and picks up her trowel. I walk over to the shade of the huge oak tree and kneel in the dirt. I start to dig a hole and hit something hard. Excited, I continue to dig to bring the object to the surface; it is small and covered with hardened dirt. I spit on it and rub it against my jeans to clean it. Finally, I see it's a shiny, flat, black rock with a point on one end. I take it to Aunt Leah and exclaim, "Look at the pretty rock I found!"

She looks at it with interest, turning it over and then looks at me. "It's an arrowhead, used by Native Americans long ago. It is very special. I'll be right back." She goes into the house and a few minutes later returns with something colorful in her hand.

Sally's voice is now speaking to me once again. "Okay Matt, I'm going to count to three. At three, open your eyes and remember what you saw. One…. two….three."

I'm now alert but still quiet as I'm focusing now on the rest of the memory and trying hard to remember it all.

"Matt, are you there? How did it go?" she asks.

"It worked! I remembered when I was about six years old, digging in the yard under the shade of a large tree and finding a black shiny rock that I thought was so pretty. I remember showing it to Aunt Leah and her telling me that it was an arrowhead. She went in the house and brought back an old Christmas can and told me it was for my treasures. That is why I would dig in the backyard so much; I was trying to find more treasures like that one."

Sally is very happy for me and encourages me to periodically practice this method to help me remember other things. After I say goodbye, I continue to sit in the swing for a while thinking about how I recently went through all my treasure cans and didn't find a complete arrowhead. I wonder what happened to it?

After this first session, I practice this technique a few more times and remember various other things that are interesting. One memory is of me making some sort of craft with paper and glue. I can remember working very hard to get something to stick to the paper but it wasn't working very well and I was getting frustrated. Aunt Leah suggested I use cardboard instead of paper which worked much better. When I finished the project, I gave it to her as a gift. She gave me a big hug and then took me out for ice cream. I have no idea why I remember that art project but it was a nice memory.

Another memory I have is of a trip with my parents to the redwoods in northern California. I must have been about nine years old at the time. I remember walking for quite a long time through the giant trees, stopping to gaze upward at the branches

Full Moon Shadow

so high in the sky, smelling the rich earthy scent of the moss, bark and lush greenery, and hearing birds singing overhead, the crunch of our steps on twigs, and squirrels calling to each other as they run around like mad. Suddenly, I felt my mom standing next to me with her arm around my shoulder asked why I was being so quiet? I remember very clearly telling her, "I am focusing on trying to remember what I see, hear and smell all around me." She smiled, gave me a big hug and walked alongside me not saying a word for the rest of the walk.

Full Moon Shadow

CJ

Darla calls instead of texting me which isn't typical. I wonder what's up? When I answer, she is very excited and asks to come over to talk to Matt and me as soon as possible. I tell Matt and we agree now is a good time and Darla says she'll be right over.

When she arrives, we meet in Matt's room with the separated piles of rocks in front of us. Darla picks up a piece of a white shell. "Matt, some of these white objects are broken polished shells that Native Americans used for trading. And some of the black rock is obsidian which was what they used to make arrowheads."

Matt is excited at this news and says, "Wow, that is interesting. I remember my Aunt Leah telling me that there used to be Native Americans in this area." Matt glances at me and then looks back at Darla and asks her, "Do you mind if I talk to CJ for a minute in private?" I'm surprised at this and Darla looks a bit taken aback too but nods okay. Matt and I get up and go into my bedroom and close the door.

"CJ, as you know, I have been working with your mom to use self-hypnosis to remember things. In the first session, I remembered finding an intact arrowhead in the backyard when I was six years old. I wanted to tell you about this memory now."

"Why's that such a big deal?" I don't get where this is going.

"I'm not sure exactly but these artifacts might have something to do with what Aunt Leah found. Or may even be tied somehow to the Shadow Man. Darla's studying anthropology, learning about different cultures; Shadow Man certainly qualifies as different!" Darla knocks on the door, we both kind of jump.

I open the door to let her into my room and say, "Sorry that we left you alone for so long." Matt looks to me and I can tell he's thinking we should tell her what is going on, the whole thing.

"Okay, what is going on?" Darla looks perplexed and a bit annoyed.

Full Moon Shadow

"Let's sit down in the living room, it is a long story." I take her hand and Matt follows. She and I sit on the couch while Matt picks up Kitty from the recliner, sits down himself and puts Kitty on his lap.

As he tells Darla the whole full moon shadow story, she goes from looking like we have lost our minds, to being scared for Matt and finally, to being worried. Finally, she says, "I'm not sure why you told me all this?"

Matt tries to explain, "I was a bit surprised when you told us the white polished shells were used for trading by Native Americans. Since I found an intact arrowhead when I was a kid, it makes sense that I found more artifacts in the backyard, even if not intact. We are wondering if all this Native American stuff could possibly tie in with the Shadow Man or with the missing object my Aunt Leah hopes I can find." She doesn't say anything but waits for Matt to continue. "Maybe your anthropology studies might help in some way?" Darla rolls her eyes and looks at us like we are both losing it.

I ask Matt, "Maybe you're trying too hard to make a connection between things you've found in the back yard and the other issues you're dealing with. As Darla mentioned, there were Native Americans throughout this area of California, so finding their artifacts in the backyard wouldn't be that strange." Matt nods in agreement and gives Darla an apologetic look.

Darla stands up and says, "Believe me, Matt, I won't tell anyone your story. Who would believe me anyway?!" She turns to go but then turns back to face Matt again. She adds, "One thing I've learned from my anthropology classes is that many strange things occur when cultural worlds collide. Especially ones that are very different from one another."

We all pause for a bit thinking about that. I can't help but think that ghosts that haunt houses are indeed, very different from the living. And things can't get much stranger than when a person is somehow able to walk into a shadow and enter another realm from their hallway wall.

Full Moon Shadow

Matt and I both stand up now to say our goodbyes to Darla. He thanks her for her efforts and she gives him a hug. I walk her to the door and she assures me that she will keep Matt's secret.

When I come back into the living room, I look at Matt and he just shrugs his shoulders and without saying another word, goes into his bedroom and quietly closes the door.

Full Moon Shadow

Matt

I contacted Elaine after I finished summarizing the yard receipts in chronological order and created a sketch of the backyard. She is now here and we are discussing my findings.

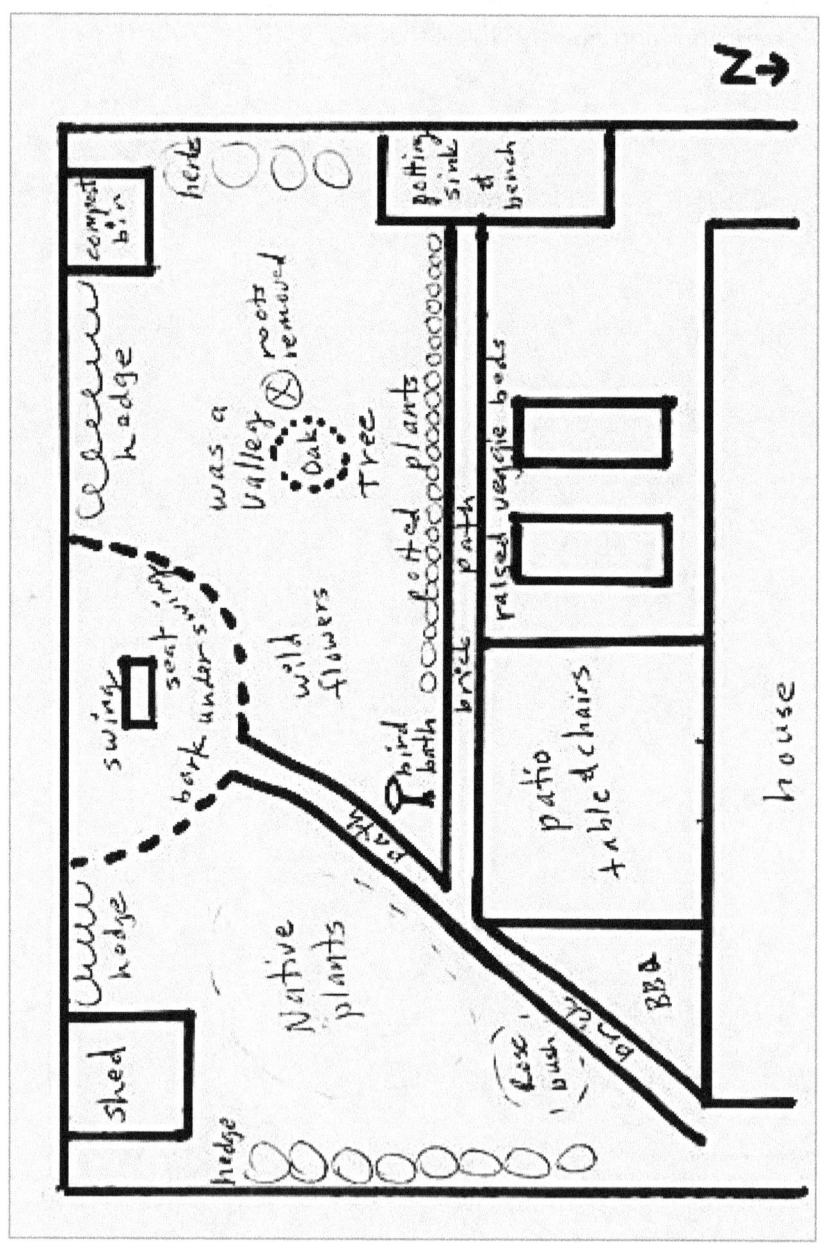

Full Moon Shadow

I explain, "I focused my efforts on the time frame a couple years before Aunt Leah had her first fall (which might have been the start of her mini strokes) up until Stan's yard efforts in September 2022."

Elaine asks "Matt, why did you stop the list in 2022?"

"There weren't any yard work receipts after that." I wonder what she's thinking.

"This project is about more than the yard work. Let's add in some other dates of important events. "When did you first notice her health declining?"

I think about this and say, "Her birthday, August 20, 2022. And her health was much worse at Thanksgiving. That's when mom called Aunt Leah's doctor. And the letter she wrote about the missing object was dated Feb 1, 2023. When did Aunt Leah tell you she saw the Shadow Man?"

"March 2023. And the next month, I saw it too." We look up full moon dates for 2023. We then add in the dates when Aunt Leah moved into the nursing home and died. Here is our summary:

Receipts for back yard work	Date
Raised beds built for veggies by dad and me	3/15/2019
Valley Oak Tree removed and stump ground	2/10/2020
Large shrubs pruned, Leah's first fall	10/10/2021
Aunt Leah's birthday, Matt notes her decline	8/20/2022
Thanksgiving, Aunt Leah's health worsening	11/20/2022
Stan removes roots after Leah's 2nd fall	12/15/2022
Aunt Leah writes letter to Matt about lost item	2/1/2023
Aunt Leah sees Shadow Man waving to her, tells Elaine	3/7/2023
Elaine sees Shadow Man waving to her	4/6/2023
Aunt Leah moves to nursing home	6/1/2023
Aunt Leah dies	1/2/2024

Full Moon Shadow

"Okay, we now have a timeline, but we still need to figure out what she found and where she might have put it. And why it is so important to take care of this thing, whatever it is." I say this and then we both look at the map again.

Elaine says very empathically, "It has to be something to do with the oak tree she had taken out and the roots that Stan cut out. She never wanted to be in the backyard after that."

"Stan told me about when Aunt Leah called him to do yard work. She twisted her ankle when her foot got caught in an old tree root. You were on vacation at the time with your family. Stan and Cara came right over to make sure she was okay and didn't need medical treatment. Aunt Leah insisted she was just sore from the fall and asked Stan to come over the next day to cut out the loose roots and fill the area with dirt."

She looks at me and says, "What did I tell you? That tree has something to do with this whole mystery." I nod in agreement.

We decide to look again for the missing object both on the book shelf in CJ's room and in the desk in the garage. We also look in all the kitchen cabinets, with Elaine insisting I use a stool to look in the back of the very highest shelves. CJ comes home and asks what's going on and decides to join in the hunt. The three of us check the garage, closets, front porch, in and under every potted plant, and under and around all the backyard plants. We then look inside and around the compost bin, the shed, raised beds, and potting bench. Nothing turns up. Frustrated and tired, we give up, at least for now. It has to be somewhere we haven't thought of yet.

Full Moon Shadow

CJ

Today, I notice Kitty standing in the hallway staring at the wall where the shadow appears. When I walk by, the poor cat jumps into the air, then runs to hide under Matt's bed. When Matt comes home from campus, I tell him about Kitty's staring at the hallway, me spooking her, and that she's now hiding. "I feel like running and hiding too when I walk past the hallway." He goes to find Kitty and sits with her for a while in the recliner talking to her. "It's okay, Kitty. It's okay now." He uses a gentle voice as he pets her. I can't help but smile.

Our busy college schedules leave little time for Matt and I to socialize much with our friends other than time spent at the coffee house or study groups like we did last quarter. But still, Darla comes over every few days to visit me but never asks to stay the night. In fact, she tells me, "After hearing about Matt going inside a shadow, I don't want to be here after dark. It's so creepy knowing what is there." She points towards the hallway.

She's here this afternoon when we hear Matt enter the house from the garage door. He goes straight into his bedroom and shuts the door. I stay in the living room as Darla knocks on Matt's door and says, "Matt, do you have a minute?"

He opens the door with a smile and says, "Sure, what's up?" I come into the hallway but stay back a bit so not to interrupt.

"CJ has been keeping me updated about your efforts to find the object your Aunt Leah misplaced. It might be some other Native American artifact. Perhaps a bigger or more significant object. I brought a library book about Native Americans with lots of drawings of things they made and traded if you want to borrow it."

"Sure, that would be great. I'm curious to learn more about Native Americans, especially their crafts. Thanks, Darla." Darla pulls the book out of her backpack and hands it to him. Matt starts to go back into his room but sees Darla's still standing there so he waits for her to continue.

Full Moon Shadow

She hesitates and then says, "I have a favor to ask you. The next full moon, I want to be here." Before Matt can respond, she rushes on to add, "I want to bring a fellow anthropology student with me, she has a special interest in Native Americans. Her name is Madison, Maddy for short. She's a first year."

Matt starts to look alarmed thinking that Darla told this person about his 'going into the shadow' experience. Darla notices right away the expression on Matt's face and quickly adds, "I didn't tell her about what happened to you, I promise. She and I were talking after class about Native American folklore and it made me think of what happened to you. You can trust her. Even if you don't want either of us here at that time, please consider meeting her sometime before then. The folklore stories she tells sound a bit like what you have experienced."

Matt first looks at Darla, then CJ, then back to Darla. "Let me think about it. I'll get back to you in a couple of days." Darla looks relieved and nods her head.

After she leaves, I ask Matt what he's thinking. He surprises me by saying, "I'm feeling that we need more help than what our parents can provide. But I have no idea who we can bring into this crazy mess that won't immediately call for us to be taken away to a loony bin." We both stare at each other for a couple of minutes while we think about this. "What do you think about Darla's request?" I shrug my shoulders. "Let's think about it some more before we decide."

Later that evening, I keep hearing Matt's words about us waiting to decide about Darla's request. I'm definitely not happy about this crazy mess either. Telling others is just asking for trouble. But I'm very glad Matt trusts me enough to value my input and that he wants me to be here to help him get through this.

Full Moon Shadow

Matt

So far this quarter, classes have been, well, not great. I realized before the spring quarter started that I would need this quarter to be as easy as possible. So, I dropped a science class and added a communication class, which is my minor anyway. I still have 16 units but even with the easier load, I'm having trouble focusing. I can't shake the Shadow Man. I haven't told anyone yet, not even CJ, but regardless of what the parents want me to do, I plan to go into the shadow again. I *HAVE to* find out what he wants from me and how I can help him. Or somehow convince him why I can't help him. If that doesn't work, I'm going to move out of Aunt Leah's house. Mom and dad might be upset about this but then they can sell the house sooner than later. I don't know why I didn't think of this before.

"CJ, I'm going for a bike ride." I call this out not even sure if he can hear me but I don't care. I know Darla is on her way over and he wants time alone with her. I feel bad he's having to "baby sit" me. What kind of a friend am I to get him involved in all this? When I'm back home from my bike ride, I go to my room and close the door so they don't feel the need to socialize with me. I don't get a chance though as Darla knocks and suggests we let someone else in on this craziness. Now I really need time to think about this. CJ doesn't have a clue if it's an okay idea or not. I go back into my room and try to study but can't. I need to talk to my parents about Darla's suggestion. I make the call and mom picks up right away.

"Mom, dad, are you both on the phone?

"We're both here, son."

"I need to know what the plan is for the full moon event. You haven't given us any details and it's driving me nuts. I can't focus on school. Just tell me. PLEASE!"

There is a long silence on the phone before dad answers. "We all think the only solution is for you to go back."

Full Moon Shadow

"What?! Go back into the shadow?" I can't believe what I'm hearing.

Dad starts to speak but before he can get a word out, I say, "That's exactly what I think too." We collectively take a breath and then dad tells me a bit more about their plan.

"We are going to meet with a couple of communication specialists when we are in Davis to consult about how we might stay connected with you while you're in there." I hadn't thought of that and am not sure how to respond when he continues. "We haven't told anyone about your experience and we don't plan to, in case that's what you're thinking."

"Actually, CJ and I told his girlfriend Darla." I can hear both mom and dad gasp over the phone and then fall silent.

"I know, you must think we're taking a huge risk but she now wants to be there during the next event."

"What? Can you trust her? Think about how we reacted." Mom's voice is shaking with worry.

I explain about Darla and her friend Madison are both anthropology majors and are used to weird tales about different cultures. Also, I assure them I haven't decided yet if we should tell Madison. I explain, "I want to meet her in person first. Even still, I'm not certain we really want to let any more people know. What do you think?"

Mom hesitates and I can hear her talking softly to dad. "If you are okay with it, we trust your judgement. But we hope that no one else has to be involved."

I agree and we say goodbye.

After I tell CJ about the phone call, I text Darla and arrange a time for us to meet her and Madison.

Full Moon Shadow

CJ

Matt and I have been talking over the last couple of days about the upcoming UC Davis Picnic Day on Saturday. Before the Shadow Man was part of our lives, Matt and I were really looking forward to this event. But now, with our parents coming, not only to attend the annual open house, but to but STAY OVER, we're kind of disappointed. However, since the next full moon is April 23, only three days after Picnic Day, we understand. After all, they're mostly going to be here to help us figure out what we can do to get rid of the Shadow Man.

My phone vibrates and I see it is mom. After I get off the phone with her, I find Matt and say, "Good news, Matt! Our parents are not wanting to be with us 24/7 on Picnic Day weekend."

"Really, we'll have the house to ourselves all weekend?" Matt is staring at me waiting for an answer.

"They DO want to go with us to watch the parade, see some of the campus, and have lunch. But by mid-afternoon, we'll be on our own. Also, they promise to let us sleep late on Sunday." Matt and I pump our fists into the air and whoop it up.

Full Moon Shadow

Matt

The meeting with Darla and Madison went really well. It turns out Madison, Maddy as she prefers to be called, is a very cute woman. She's a bit on the fuller side with blond, curly hair, golden brown eyes and a few freckles across her cheeks and nose. I can't help but appreciate that she's a bit shorter than me and has a wonderful smile. When she laughs, her entire face lights up. It makes me want to put my arms around her and feel her joy. But it's too early for that. She does seem to like me though and wasn't alarmed when CJ, Darla, and I told her about my full moon shadow experience. She took it in stride and proceeded to tell us a few amazing folklore stories about Native Americans and other indigenous groups that made my shadow experience seem mild. Of course, the folklore tales are just tales, not real. It was nice of her though to suggest maybe there is some truth to the tales. "Who knows," we all said laughing. CJ and I told both Darla and Maddy they can attend the full moon if they truly feel comfortable with what may happen.

* * *

Picnic Day slayed! Our parents enjoyed the festivities, meeting some of our professors and classmates. We picnicked in the redwood grove with food brought by Sally and cookies baked by Cara, Stan's wife. Elaine was purposely out of town on Picnic Day to avoid the madness so she wasn't there to join us. I told mom a few days ago about Cara's suggestion for a Celebration of Life for Aunt Leah. She and mom must have made a date to meet Saturday morning as Cara showed up at 9 am. When I answered the door, she handed me a basket full of her delicious chocolate chip cookies and then sat and talked with mom at length over coffee.

By 3 pm, our parents were off to meet with technical experts they had appointments with and CJ and I had the rest of the day to ourselves. We meet up with friends, including Darla and Maddy, and stay till dark listening to the annual college band competition before heading back to the house. CJ fixes quesadillas for dinner and I make a pitcher of margaritas. Maddy and I talk for hours about everything and nothing. It just seems so natural to talk to her that time flies by. I hadn't noticed that CJ and Darla had disappeared until they suddenly reappear and Darla asks Maddy if she's about ready to go.

"Yes, I'm ready." Maddy looks at me and smiles. Darla goes into CJ's room to gather her things. I walk Maddy to the door and we stop and look at each other not knowing what to say. I notice her brown eyes are flecked with gold.

I manage to ask her, "Are you seeing anyone? I mean, I would like to take you out after all of this is over, if you're interested." I find myself getting flushed.

"I'm available and interested." She smiles at me and steps a bit closer.

I put by arms around her waist and give her a short, gentle kiss. She puts her arms around me and we share a longer more meaningful kiss. When we part, I can't help but sigh aloud and she stifles a giggle. With a gentle hand, she brushes away a lock of my hair that strayed across my eyes. I feel the electricity of her touch that takes my breath away. She must have felt it too as I notice her cheeks are now pink. She turns away to join Darla who is now in front of the open garage getting on her bike. As I watch CJ close the garage door, I see he's grinning from ear to ear.

* * *

Now it's Sunday and CJ and I sleep in till about 11 am. Our parents arrive shortly after we get up and are eager to talk about their plan. My dad is trying to tell me something but my mind keeps drifting back to Maddy. I guess that's good as meeting her has kept me from being too stressed. Dad's voice penetrates my thoughts and I turn to him to focus on what he's saying.

"Matt, we talked to experts about how people are able to communicate when they are in mines or shafts with people above ground. Unfortunately, cell phones and other devices won't work without special receivers already set in the area. So those ideas won't work. Instead, we hope to record what you hear in the shadow. You could use the voice memo feature on a cell phone. Or you could go old school and use a mini tape recorder. It might be less likely to run out of battery." He puts two devices on the table.

I pick up the mini tape player and stare at it. Wow, really interesting. Then I pick up the cell phone and recognize that it's dad's phone. I look at him questioningly and he says, "I brought myself a new phone. You can use my old one for this project."

I nod and say, "I would like to practice using each."

Dad smiles at me and agrees. "I was hoping you would say that. Can you think of places to go this afternoon that has lots of background noise and we can try them out? Or perhaps you would rather try with CJ?"

CJ and I look at each other and smile. However, CJ nods ever so slightly towards my dad. "Dad, I think you and I should try them out together." Dad beams at me.

After I down some coffee and a quick snack, the two of us go downtown and stand around a coffee house near the outdoor tables. He has the tape recorder in his pocket turned on. I have the cell phone voice-memo app turned on in my pocket. We carry on a conversation walking around all the people talking, drinking and eating. There is a lot of laughter, clanking of dishes, and chairs scooting in and out. After about ten minutes of this, we switch recording devices and walk towards a busy intersection with bikes, scooters, and people talking and walking. Again, we carry on a conversation, trying to use our normal voices.

We walk away from the noise to an unoccupied area across the street to listen to the recordings; they are okay, not great. Definitely, the person carrying the device is heard more clearly than anyone else. They both were easy to use. The last test is with me carrying both devices, one in each pocket, and talking to dad as we ride our bikes along a street with less stop signs so we can ride at a steady pace. We think the movement will somewhat simulate me falling down a chute or walking down a passage. There are others biking beside us and cars driving by as we ride. We try to talk to each other as we go. We compare these results. They are both equally bad. Disappointed, we head home.

Mom and Sally greet us at the door with questions on their faces. I hear CJ, Darla, and Maddy in the kitchen and I'm anxious to greet Maddy but make myself stop and listen as dad relays the news. "Neither recording device worked great for hearing anyone far away but they could pick up the person carrying it alright when the background noise wasn't too loud." I nod in agreement and excuse myself.

Maddy and CJ are putting something that smells delicious into a serving bowl and Darla is setting the table. They look up at me when I come in. Maddy speaks first, "You're just in time for lunch." She smiles and my heart melts. CJ and Darla look at each other grinning.

Lunch consists of a chicken stew made by Maddy and CJ, salad made by Darla, and homemade cornbread made by Sally. Mom comes in the kitchen with a plate of cupcakes courtesy of Elaine who follows mom carrying with a pitcher of lemonade. Soon we are all sitting at the dining room table eating and laughing, acting like it's a normal gathering with nothing big happening in two days.

The conversation finally turns to why they are all here. Sally, mom and Elaine tell us they searched for Aunt Leah's missing object while dad and I were gone but didn't find anything. They ask me to go over again about my last encounter with the Shadow Man and I reluctantly oblige. I keep it brief and they are all fine with that. Relieved, we get up from the table and the ladies go out on the patio to enjoy the warmth of the spring day.

Now that CJ's new bed is here, dad, CJ and I move the old hide-a-bed to the garage and then assemble the new one. When we are done, CJ and dad head out to the patio while I go into the kitchen. I hear Sally and mom go into CJ's room to make up the bed. I'm about to join the others on the patio when I hear a loud clatter from CJ's room. Mom comes into the kitchen and asks, "Where's your dad?"

"On the patio," I reply and we both go outside.

She walks up to dad and says, "There is something behind the bookcase. We bumped into it and heard something clatter to the floor. You know how heavy it is, we need help moving it away from the wall." Dad nods and he, CJ and I go into CJ's room while mom follows. Sally is sitting on the computer chair out of the way and mom goes to stand next to her. Everyone else has followed us from the patio and are now in the hallway looking in, all curious about what is going on. Dad, CJ and I manage to move one side of the bookcase away from the wall about eight inches, enough for dad to reach behind and recover what fell. We see the puzzled look on his face as he picks up the object and turns to face us. He places his hand out for us to see it. At first, none of us can tell what he's holding. Finally, Darla breaks the silence.

"It's part of a jaw bone. A human jaw." Maddy nods in agreement.

I take it from dad and say, "This must be what Aunt Leah misplaced, it has to be." They look puzzled at first but slowly nod in agreement. I place it on the bed.

Elaine says, "No wonder she didn't tell me what she found. It is a strange thing to find in your backyard and definitely creepy."

Dad signals for CJ and I to help him move the other side of the bookcase away from the wall. On the floor, I see the second half of the jaw bone. I pick it up and put it next to the other jaw piece on the bed. Everyone is staring at the two pieces of a human jaw bone. However, I see that there's something else behind the bookcase. I reach down and pull out a piece of cardboard. When I turn it over, I find it has been painted blue and glued to its center is a black arrowhead with printed writing below it. I put it on the top of the bookcase to share later. I look at everyone staring at the jaw bone pieces and clear my throat to get their attention.

Full Moon Shadow

"Aunt Leah must have put the jawbone on top of her bookcase to give her time to think about what to do about her discovery. Maybe it was already broken in two. Whatever condition it was in when she found it, it would have been very shocking to her, especially with her illness. When she was healthy, I'm sure she would have called the police right away. But given the mini strokes she had been having over the last year, she was probably confused about what was the best thing to do." I stop to let that sink in and notice mom and Elaine are clinging to one another. "However, after a few days, she must have forgotten what she had found, and more importantly, where she had put it. Or perhaps by then, it had already fallen behind the bookcase so she couldn't see it. She definitely remembered there was something she found that needed to be taken care of, even if she couldn't find it. That is why she wrote me that letter."

CJ adds, "It must have been wedged between the bookcase and the wall. It's a good thing the bookcase got bumped today or we might not have ever found it." He picks up both pieces of the jaw and carries them into the living room. We all follow him and sit down. CJ hands the jaw pieces to Maddy and Darla. After they examine them, they offer to pass them around but no one else wants to hold them, so Darla places the bones gently on the coffee table.

Maddy says, "As you may know, there were Native Americans that lived here long ago. They lived throughout Yolo County and in neighboring areas. Grave sites have been discovered during various construction projects over the years, some only blocks from here."

Dad interjects, "But it could be anyone, really. Just finding parts of a human body doesn't mean it's a Native American. Or that a whole body is buried in the back yard." At that, mom and Elaine both gasp at the thought.

Darla adds, "Animals could have found the jawbone of a buried body somewhere else and brought it to Leah's backyard and reburied it. Regardless, the authorities need to be informed. They are trained in dealing with this."

Elaine gets weepy and says, "I'm sure that is what Leah intended to do but she must have been confused. Her memory was all in pieces. Sometimes, she didn't even remember my name." Mom hands her a tissue and takes one for herself.

Maddy explains that the authorities will investigate and look in the yard for other remains. When appropriate, they will contact the Native American Heritage Commission, who, if they accept the body as theirs, will have the ultimate say in where the remains end up. They are very private about the location of their buried dead.

I think back to my list of backyard receipts. Aunt Leah must have found the jaw bone when she tripped in the back yard. Perhaps that is what broke the bone in two. Whatever the reason, she was very upset and asked Stan to cut out the root and then cover the area with soil. She knew she wanted the trip hazard gone and didn't want to find anything else unexpected in her beloved backyard. I see Darla and CJ looking at me. They are thinking the same thing.

Dad says what everyone is already thinking. "I suggest waiting to call the police until Matt gets back from the shadow. Once we know he's okay, we will call them." No one argues with this. After that troubling find of a jawbone, a broken jawbone at that, no one wants to talk much. Darla and Maddy leave soon afterwards.

Full Moon Shadow

CJ

Monday and Tuesday, Matt and I go to classes even though I'm sure neither of us were as focused as we should have been. When we come home afterwards, it's a bit like being in high school with our parents there. Both nights, the parents cook us dinner which is nice. On Tuesday night, the night of the full moon, no one eats much, especially Matt. While we push our food around on our plates, we attempt to make small talk. Suddenly, Matt stands up and announces to everyone, "I'm sure there is an entire body buried in the back yard and that it is somehow connected to the Shadow Man." At first, everyone looks shocked at his announcement but then they nod their heads.

The parents look at one another nodding and then mom says, "We have been talking about it since finding the jawbone and agree that's very likely the case. They look at Matt as it is obvious since he's still standing, he has more to say.

Matt continues. "I want you to know, tonight I will try my best to get this thing resolved with the Shadow Man. But regardless, once the police are contacted about our finding of a jawbone, it will be a zoo here, and who knows for how long. CJ and I talked and we want to move out." Derek starts to speak but Matt interrupts and continues. "We have been looking for an apartment to sublet. There are a few available now and many more will be open when the quarter ends but they're all furnished. However, CJ knows a couple that graduated the end of March and moved out of the area. They're hoping to find someone to take over their lease as paying rent for two apartments is killing them. It's a two bedroom which would be perfect for us." He lets that hang in the air. "Neither of us want to live in a house with a dead body or body parts buried in the yard." Matt sits back down and everyone starts talking.

Derek says, "Matt, CJ, that makes perfect sense. I'm glad you found a solution about where to move. We will help, of course, with making the arrangements, dealing with the police, all that."

He turns to Brenda and says, "It's good we all took the entire week off. We are going to be busy."

When I stand up, they all look up at me surprised. I say cheerfully, "Let's go out for ice cream!" To my surprise, they all agree and stand up too. Some leave the room to get ready to go while others work to clear the table. Topics of discussion now are what is the best ice cream place in town, if anyone prefers frozen yogurt (no one), etc. As we enter the living room on our way to the front door, we find Matt standing by the couch holding what looks like a piece of blue painted cardboard. He tilts the object for us to better see it.

We now see it's child's art project with an arrowhead glued to the center with writing beneath that says:

"Thank you for the can to keep my tresures Love, Matty."

Brenda takes it from him and admires her son's childhood art work then asks, "Wherever did you find this?"

Matt replies, "It was behind the bookcase." Everyone smiles.

I go over to Matt and tell him, "You finally found out what happened to the first arrowhead." He nods and says, "I misspelled *treasure*."

"Dude, you were what, six?" I punch him softly on the shoulder. He shakes his head, finally breaking into a grin.

Brenda gives the two of us a glance and then says, "I'm sure she treasured this!" She carefully places it on the coffee table and heads towards the door. As we leave for ice cream, I know what I want to get: a banana split.

* * *

Using the internet and by watching the moon the last few nights, we figure out that during the next full moon, April 23, it will likely begin to shine in the bathroom window about 3 am. We also notice the moon stays in position to cast a shadow on the bathroom wall for about 2 hours before it's too low to shine into the window.

It is now midnight and we are all sitting at the table going over the last details. Brenda has removed the curtains from the bathroom window. Matt is dressed in his sweat pants and a short-sleeved tee shirt like the last time he went into the shadow. This time though, he's wearing sneakers instead of being barefoot. Elaine, Darla and Maddy are planning to arrive around 1 am.

Matt's phone rings and he picks it up and scowls. He says something we can't quite hear. After he hangs up, he turns to us and says, "Darla and Maddy have been discussing the finding of the jawbone and what it might mean. They are worried about me going into the shadow again and aren't sure they want to be here, at least not until I'm back and they know I'm okay." Matt is rubbing his forehead and trying to keep composed but looks like he's going to combust.

Brenda says, "Maybe they'll feel better if they know most of us will be waiting in the living room. Do you want me to call one of them for you?" Matt shakes his head and appears even more frustrated at the thought of her calling his friends. Mom goes over to Matt and speaks quietly to him. Matt nods and goes into the living room and sits down in the recliner, closes his eyes, and takes a few deep breaths. I recognize he's using deep breathing exercises to calm himself. My mom taught me those exercises too a long time ago. Everyone continues talking at the table letting Matt have time to himself.

After a few minutes, he opens his eyes and rejoins us at the dining room table. He looks at his mom like she's the only one there and says, "You asked me a question that I couldn't answer before, about when I went into the shadow last month and fainted in the bathroom. You wanted to know how I got from the bathroom to my bed after fainting and I told you I didn't know." Everyone is staring at him, waiting for him to continue. "Sally taught me how to use self-hypnosis to help me remember things. After a recent session, I remembered and want to tell you now. But I don't want

Full Moon Shadow

you to interrupt, okay?!" Brenda slowly nods in agreement and then Matt looks at the rest of us and repeats, "Okay?" From his tone, we can tell he is very nervous. We all murmur our agreement. He sits down at the table and takes a deep breath before he starts.

Matt directs his attention back to his mom and begins. "Aunt Leah came to help me. I heard her voice when I was regaining consciousness on the bathroom floor. I remember feeling so very, very cold. She said, 'Oh Matty, let me help you up. You need to get into bed now.' First, she helped me into a sitting position and then supported me while I pulled myself up to standing. I stood holding onto the sink a few minutes waiting for my legs to stop shaking. Then, very slowly, leaning on her for support, we made our way into my room."

"She helped me into the bed and pulled the covers up around me and tucked them in like she did when I was a kid on a cold winter night. I was shivering uncontrollably. She sat down on the bed next to me and said, 'I'll stay with you for a bit. Okay, Matty?' I couldn't speak but I tried to nod. She gently used her hand to brush my hair away from my face and then touched my cheek. I felt her hand on my face and the weight of her sitting on the bed next to me. I looked at her not really believing she was there. Eventually, I stopped shaking so much and my eyes closed. I felt the weight of the bed shift when she got up to go. I wanted to say thank you but I couldn't open my eyes, I was so exhausted and fell asleep."

Matt's face now looks moist and he struggles to maintain control. He takes a couple of deep breaths before he continues. "When I woke up, I had no memory of her having come to help me. I didn't even remember going into the shadow. I was just confused about everything. It took several minutes before I was awake enough to think straight at all. Once I started remembering, I texted CJ, then you and not long after that, Elaine showed up." He breaks eye contact with his mom and looks at us all. He seems nervous about how everyone will react to his memory.

Full Moon Shadow

Brenda goes to Matt and holds out her arms. She is crying, her face is completely wet with tears. "Matty, of course Aunt Leah came to help you. Of course, of course." As Brenda leans over Matt to try to embrace him, he stands up and hugs her tight. No one else says anything as we are all moved.

We take a break before resuming the discussion about the final details. Once we are settled again back at the table, Matt tells everyone, "I think I should put the jaw bone in my pocket to take with me into the shadow."

Brenda says, "But you might lose it when or if you fall down that shaft." Brenda looks at Derek and mom for their opinions.

Derek says, "If you have the jaw in one pocket, what recording device are you going to take in the other pocket? You can't take two in one pocket!" Derek is trying to not sound irritated but failing. "We want to be able to hear…"

Mom raises her voice to interrupt Derek and says, "Just take one half the jaw in one pocket and the recording device in the other."

I can't stand it any longer and say "Let Matt decide! He's the one going through this." They all shut up.

Matt looks at me and gives me a small smile in thanks. "Dad, I think I will take my cell phone as I can lock it once I turn on voice memo and it should be able to stand the heat. I will put the cell in a zip-lock bag. I tried it and it works just fine in a baggie." He turns to his mom and says, "In the other pocket, I will take one half the jaw bone wrapped in something so it won't fall out. Can you please take a photo of both jaw pieces from all angles. Then I will take the smaller half with me." Brenda nods and gets up from the table to get her phone. Matt goes to his room and comes back a few seconds later.

Mom asks Matt if he remembers the questions he wants to ask the Shadow Man; he nods. Brenda comes back with the jaw bone pieces and hands the smaller piece to Matt. He says, "I grabbed an old sock from my dresser to put the bone in." He then puts the bone inside the old sock and places it deep into his sweatpants pocket, and jumps up and down to make sure it stays put. He then gets the cell phone ready. I can see the battery is fully charged and he has the voice memo app open. He puts it in a baggie and seals it up. Everyone watches as he does all these preparations in silence. We all move into the living room to wait until time.

When the doorbell rings, we all jump a bit. I go to answer it and Darla, Maddy, and Elaine are all there. They look rather nervous as they come into the living room one by one. When Matt sees Maddy, he looks very relieved. He gives each of them a hug and kisses Maddy on the cheek. "I'm glad you're here. You can wait in the living room while I'm inside the shadow. CJ and dad will monitor the bathroom for when I come back." They all nod and silently find a place to sit down.

* * *

The full moon can now be seen from the bathroom window and there is a shadow on the hallway wall in the shape of an open door. Derek, Matt and I are in the bathroom looking at it. I'm sitting on the toilet out of the way, Derek and Matt are both standing in the doorway, directly in front of the shadow. I am looking for the Shadow Man but don't see anyone there. Derek has his new cell phone mounted on a tripod located next to the toilet; it's directed at the shadow. It is ready to record; it's my job to start it when things begin to happen.

Derek is nervous and can't seem to stop talking to Matt. "We will be here for you, waiting. If you don't come back within 30 minutes, I will come in and find you." Matt is nodding his head ever so slightly all the while looking into the shadow. Abruptly, he turns away from his dad and looks at me and winks. He then turns back around to face his dad.

Matt asks him, "Where's Kitty? I don't want her to follow me in this time." Derek turns to me and I shrug my shoulders. Derek holds up a finger signaling just a minute and goes into the living room. We can hear Elaine telling him that Kitty is sound asleep in Matt's room with the door closed.

Full Moon Shadow

Derek comes back into the bathroom just as Matt's leg and then foot disappear into the wall. He's in the Shadow Man's world now.

Full Moon Shadow

Matt

As I watch the Shadow Man appear, my dad is talking in a hurried nervous voice. Dad doesn't appear to see the image in the shadow or he's just not wanting to see it. I'm glad that CJ and I had a contingency plan to get my dad out of the bathroom so I could go in without my dad freaking out. When my dad leaves the room to check on Kitty, I see the Shadow Man wave for me to follow him. I take out the cell phone, press RECORD on the voice memo app and then lock the phone. I give CJ a quick a thumbs up before stepping briskly into the warmth of the shadow.

I'm now in the darkness once again. The Shadow Man is the only source of light and generates warmth as he takes long strides down the path. Neither of us try to speak as we both know our voices will only sound like the wind while in the passage way. It seems we walk for a longer distance than the last time I followed him into the shadow. I am hoping the voice memo function stays active for a long enough period as for right now, there is nothing for it to record and I think we've been walking for about five minutes. The path has been gradually sloping downward and it's getting steeper and harder to keep from falling. If I could see the ground, it wouldn't be so hard to keep my balance.

After several wobbly steps, I almost fall but before I do, the Shadow Man takes my arm. It burns as it did before and I try to pull away from him. Instead, he wraps his arms around me and I'm encased by his light. We fall down a shaft but this time, it is short and we soon land on a soft surface. I don't lose my balance when he releases me and back away from him. It is tricky though, as it is still dark and I can only manage to put a few yards between us. Leon Hoke, if that's really his name, goes from being a light silhouette into an intense hot, bright light. I have to close my eyes from the intensity of the light. I can feel him getting brighter and hotter and suddenly, I hear a loud popping noise. I open my eyes to see what happened.

Full Moon Shadow

It is no longer too dark to see and I look around. I don't see the bright Shadow Man anywhere and definitely don't feel his heat. I can now see the area where we landed; it's a large meadow of soft grass with tiny flowers everywhere. At the edge of the meadow are trees and shrubs. I kind of expected to be in the same place as my last visit so I'm surprised at the new surroundings. I look skyward and see the bright full moon and lots of stars. There doesn't appear to be a cloud in the sky. I notice the sound of rushing water nearby and look around for the source. I walk towards the shrubs and see behind them a fast-moving stream. It must have stormed recently as the water is very dirty and filled with branches, twigs and leaves tumbling quickly downstream. When I look upstream, I see the Shadow Man. He's no longer bright light but muted colors of tan and beige, phasing in and out, just like my last visit. He is about 50 feet away and staring at me. He says, "So you decided to come and speak with me again." His voice is strong and clear, unlike last time when he first spoke in a garbled, hoarse voice.

I walk closer to him and reply, "Yes, I came to help." This time, it's MY voice that's scratchy and soft. I clear it and start again. "My name is Matt. I came back to find out what you need me to do for you. Please let me know how I can help."

He walks towards me and stops when he's about ten feet away. "I want you to tell me why your people killed me. And why now, even after death, you do not let me rest in peace?" He comes closer to me now and I see his hands are in fists.

"Mr. Hoke, I'm not sure why you think we killed you? But..."

***"WHAT DID YOU CALL ME?!"** He's now yelling at me.*

"Last time I followed you into the shadow, I thought you said your name was Leon Hoke?" He doesn't reply but just stares at me. "Maybe I heard you wrong, your voice was very soft and garbled when you first spoke to me."

I can tell he's thinking about the last time. He relaxes and seems to give me a small smile. I'm relieved that he's not yelling anymore. *"Leon Hoke – HA! The last time you came, I told you to call me 'Leaning Oak.' I gave that as my name as you could not pronounce my name."* He motions for me to come closer to him. As I move slowly towards him, he sits down on a fallen tree. He motions for me to also sit on the fallen tree. I do as he wants but I sit as far away as I can from him, about ten feet.

"Your people brought sickness to my people, many of my family died. We tried to live in peace and let the newcomers share the land with us. More of your people came though and our tribe kept having to move. Eventually, there were so few of us left, your people wanted us to move to a place they said would be ours, ours alone. A few from our tribe went to see this place and it was a not good location. There was no stream, no oak trees, no game for us to hunt or plants we could use. When our people reported this to our tribe, we told your people we would not move." Leaning Oak pauses and seems to want me to comment.

"I'm sorry for what happened to your people. You had the right to stay in your home and not be told to move. Please know that happened long before I was born, long before my parents or even my grandparents were born." I try to express sorrow in my voice for what happened to him and his people.

Leaning Oak nods curtly. *"When we refused to leave, your men started shooting at us. We ran as fast as we could. My brother and a few others managed to get away. The others... I don't know what happened to them. One of the men chasing us caught up with me and pushed me into the stream. It was full of fast running water, just like that stream is now."* He stands up and points to it. It takes all my willpower to stay sitting and not get up and run.

"I'm so sorry that happened. As I told you, that was before my time. I can't control the past. Certainly, it was wrong of them to try to hurt you and your people." I do my best to keep looking in his eyes and try to not show that I'm very nervous and shaking.

"But your family can control what is happening in THEIR LAND, IN THEIR YARD." He stands up and starts to walk towards me so I also stand and take a few steps away from him.

Full Moon Shadow

"I don't know what you're talking about?" I am uncertain what he wants. "Why don't you tell me what you think my family did wrong? And what does it have to do with you?"

That must have been the wrong thing to say as now Leaning Oak has balled up his hands into fists again. "Didn't you find some of my things in the back yard? Where do you think they came from?" He is even closer to me now.

"Yes, I found an arrowhead when I was a child and then found other things like shiny rocks, polished shells and twigs with moss. I was just a small boy. I didn't find out until recently that Native Americans used polished shells." I have now moved further away from him but behind me are downed trees, shrubs, and the stream of rushing water. He still looks angry.

He stops advancing towards me and looks thoughtful. "I didn't die when I was pushed into the water but my face hit a log when I landed in the water. Somehow, I managed to make it to the side of the stream and I grabbed hold of a tree root at the water's edge. I could feel blood coming from my mouth and forehead." He walks back over and sits back down on the fallen tree then continues. "After a long time, my brother found me and pulled me out of the water. He tried to get us both to a safe place but I couldn't walk very far, even with his help. I'd lost too much blood and was very weak."

"I died in the middle of a field next to a young oak tree that was slightly leaning towards the northeast. My brother buried me next to that tree, deep in the earth as is our custom. On my body, he placed the few possessions I had with me; my trading beads, a few arrowheads, and arrows." He hangs his head and sits quietly for a few minutes. "That is where my brother put my body to rest, to be left alone for all eternity." His voice remains tight as he tries to stay calm.

"That sounds awful. I'm so sorry that happened to you." He nods his head and continues to look at me. "Now, please listen as I tell you what happened in my Aunt Leah's backyard. When she bought the house, an oak tree was already there. She loved that

tree. As the tree got older, it started to lean more each year till finally, she had to have it cut down."

"This I know, that is why I told you to call me Leaning Oak."

"Let me explain, the workers cut down the tree and ground the stump down to below the surface to make it level with the ground. That is what likely disturbed your grave." I keep talking as he seems to be listening closely to my words. "The roots that remained started to decay and poke up through the ground surface. Not long ago, she tripped in her yard over a tree root, an oak tree root. When she fell, she found a bone. A human bone. She found it in the same area that I found the arrowhead and shells in the yard when I was a child. This happened not too long before she died. She put the bone somewhere and then couldn't remember where she put it. Her memory was failing from strokes she'd been having and she wanted me to find it for her, to put things right. She wants me to do the right thing now."

Leaning Oak replies, "I know that she uncovered my grave when she had the workers remove the tree." He stands up now. "But she had no right to take a bone from my grave. NO RIGHT!" He is yelling now and his fists are raised ready for a fight. He starts coming towards me. His tan and gray color pulsates faster as he gets nearer to me.

Standing up, I continue to try to explain, "She didn't know what to do with the bone she found. She didn't know what to think, what to do. She had been forgetting things, even her best friend's name." I'm slowing backing away from him. I'm getting closer to the many downed trees and branches behind me and the stream just beyond that.

"Please believe me. She didn't know what to do with your bone. She had the area covered up right after finding it though. She put the bone in her office and then forgot where she put it. We just found it a couple of days ago. It had fallen behind a bookcase." He is looking vicious and getting closer to me. I have no idea what to say to appease him. "I have it with me. Do you want it?"

Full Moon Shadow

*He stops and looks at me in shock. This time when he speaks, is sounds like a low growl. "You have a bone of mine with you! You are just as bad as your aunt and will pay for this. Just like I said before, you and your people have no respect for us. **NO RESPECT AT ALL.**" He lunges for me and I side step and narrowly escape his clutches. I turn to run but my foot gets tangled in a tree root and I fall down. As I struggle to get up, he comes and stands over me. He looks down at me curiously as the sock has comes out of my pocket and the jaw bone is poking out of it. He reaches down and picks it up, looking at it for a long minute. When he realizes what it is, he drops it like it is fire. He leans back his torso with his arms outstretched and opens his mouth in a silent roar which seems even worse than when he yells. He then turns to face me and slowly, deliberately, reaches down with both hands for my neck. I continue to struggle as hard as I can to try to free my foot from the tree root. As I pull, the root is pulling me tighter and I can't break free.*

Just when I feel his fingers start to close in on my neck, several flashes of lightning fill the sky followed by the deafening sound of thunder. Leaning Oak suddenly stands tall and takes a step away from me. He puts his hands on his hips and looks up at the sky and full moon overhead for several seconds. While he's distracted, I'm able to sit up and use my hands to untangle my foot from the tree root. Once free, but still on the ground, I glance up at him to see if he's coming at me again. I'm surprised to note that instead, he's gazing at his hands, turning them over and examining them closely. I look at them too and see they're now lighter than they were before the lightning and thunder. His whole body is lighter in color now and I can feel warmth once again emanating from him. He looks upward at the sky again and then back at me, his expression sorrowful and resigned.

He is calm now and puts out one hand to help me up. "Come on, let's talk. My time here is almost up. Soon I will rejoin the spirit world." After he helps me up, we go back and sit on the log again. Neither of us speaks for a while. Finally, he says, "Your aunt fell?" I nod. He and I both look back at the root I just tripped over. He then goes to retrieve the piece of jaw bone he dropped moments before. He looks at it for a few seconds and then hands it back to me.

"Can you do something for me?" He looks into my eyes as if searching for my soul.

I meet his gaze and say, "It depends on what you want. And then, if it's reasonable, I will do my very best."

"I appreciate your honesty. It has been more than a hundred years since I joined the spirit world. It is peaceful when my body is at rest and that is where I want to be again for all eternity. When my grave was disturbed, my spirit started to stir. And then, when your aunt picked up my bone, my spirit was no longer at peace. I am still with the spirit world but I am not in the same peaceful, restful place I was before."

"What is THIS place?" I motion around us to indicate where we are right now. I'm hopeful that he won't get angry again for me asking this question.

"This place is where I am allowed to communicate with the living. You might call it an intermittent place. It only occurs on nights with a full moon. And only the living that are willing to enter can come here. The communication is only allowed when there are things that need to be put right. Because my grave has been disturbed, my soul can't rest. I need your help to fix this problem. I want my soul to be able to rest once again."

He looks at me to see if I understand. And then he turns away from me avoiding my gaze and continues. "If I hurt you though, I cannot go back to the peaceful place; the spirits will not allow it." He bows his head and then finally, looks at me directly and says, "I should not have tried to harm you."

I nod and say, "Please, tell me what you want me to do."

"Can you put my body, ALL OF IT, somewhere that it won't be disturbed again? That way I can be at peace once again."

Full Moon Shadow

"I will contact our local authorities. They will work with representatives from your people to find a final resting place for your body. This place will not be shared with our people, only the tribal council representatives will know your final resting place." He listens calmly to this and then nods his head. "I can't guarantee that this will happen but from what I've been told, this is what our law says should happen when a body is found."

"You will do this then? Contact the right people? And they will make sure to rebury my body, all of me?" He nods his head towards his bone in my hand.

I place his jaw bone back into my pocket along with the loose sock and then tell him, "From what I know about the procedures, our people try very hard to respect your customs about burial. The tribal commission keeps the information about burial locations confidential. My family will not be involved in the burial process, only your people and those who value your customs." He nods and lifts his head towards the heavens once again as there is a short flash of lightning but no thunder.

"I need to tell you though; it may take some time for our authorities and your tribunal leaders to make decisions. It may take months before your body is reburied. And many people have to work together to arrange for this to happen. I have no control over the process."

Leaning Oak thinks about this and replies, "A few months is not long compared to eternity. I agree to your plan."

"Can I ask you a question now?" He looks at me waiting. "Will you no longer come inside the shadow of the house to see us?"

He is silent for at least a full minute before he replies, "I'm expecting you to keep your word so I won't need to." I nod thinking that is probably the best I can hope for from him.

"I will take you home now." We both stand. I can see he is lighter in color now, shimmering, and the heat emanating from his body is getting stronger. "I need to hurry so we will return differently

Full Moon Shadow

this time; I promise you won't be harmed." I stand as still as I can but I am shaking with nervousness.

Leaning Oak puts his arms overhead and palms together pointing towards the full moon. He turns into bright light and once again is emanating extraordinary heat. As I close my eyes against the brightness, I feel his arms encase me, burning me. I can't help but struggle against the pain. Still holding me, he runs and jumps into the flowing, rushing stream. As we hit the water, the burning sensation where he is holding me changes to icy cold. I see steam rising up all around us like when lava flows into the sea. When we are about to go under water, I hold my breath. We sink deep, deep into the water. Just when I think I can no longer hold my breath, I emerge alone with a burst of water. I'm now on the hallway floor in front of the bathroom dripping wet. I take a huge breath of precious air and notice dad and CJ are both staring at me. CJ is too stunned to speak. Dad says, almost in a whisper, "He's back!" Then he says it again, slightly louder, "Brenda, he's back."

Full Moon Shadow

CJ

Derek comes back into the hallway and sees Matt's leg disappear into the wall. From the look on his face, I can tell he's about to pass out so I rush over and help him sit down on the toilet seat.

He puts his head in his hands bending forward over his knees for a few minutes before sitting upright and then looks at me accusingly. "Why didn't he wait till I came back?" He has some color back in his face now but is shaking from the shock.

"I think he knew it would be hard for you to see him disappear like that. Believe me, it was shocking for me to witness too! I don't think, until that exact moment, I really quite believed he really could go into the shadow."

He says nothing for a few minutes and then notices that his cell phone is recording. "I think we should let it continue to record so we will know how long he's gone and we don't miss him coming back." He looks at me to see if I agree with him.

"That sounds reasonable. Let's take turns so one of us stays here at all times to make sure we don't miss anything. Are you okay if I go in the other room and tell the others he's gone?" Derek nods and resumes resting his head in his hands. I quickly leave the room.

Everyone looks up expectantly when I enter the living room. When I tell them Matt has entered the shadow, Darla and Maddy turn pale while Elaine, Brenda and mom all calmly acknowledge that Matt's no longer in our realm. I give Darla a hug and bring a tissue box to Maddy who is silently crying. I rub her back which makes her tears turn to sobs. Now mom comes over and talks reassuringly to her and Darla. Once I see that the girls are calmer, I return to the bathroom. Derek is now standing and motions for me to take his place. We take turns like this about every 15 minutes. What little conversation that takes place is only at a whisper. The house seems unnervingly quiet. I keep checking my phone and see Matt's been in there an hour now.

Full Moon Shadow

At my next turn to sit with the ladies, Kitty wakes from her nap in Matt's room and is scratching at the door trying to get out. We don't want her to enter the shadow like she did last time but her scratching is driving us nuts. Elaine decides to go and sit with Kitty. I go to help as it takes two of us to open the door without letting Kitty sneak past us. Once I get the door closed, I join Derek in the bathroom. Just when he's about to leave the bathroom, we hear a loud rushing sound and there's Matt, soaking wet, back through the shadow and in our realm once again. Derek tries to say, "He's back, Brenda, he's back." But his voice is raspy as he is holding back tears of relief seeing his son in one piece once again.

We both help Matt to his feet. He tries to talk but he's coughing. I hand him a glass of water while Derek gives him towels to mop up water dripping from his clothes. The others must have heard the rush of water or coughing as Brenda rushes in and put her arms around Matt sobbing with joy not caring that she's getting all wet. Matt hugs her back briefly and then goes to sit on the toilet. He takes several deep breaths and sips more water. Derek puts one arm around Matt partly to steady him but I think mostly to reassure himself that he's really here. I'm sitting on the edge of the bathtub and Brenda stands next to me. Mom, Darla and Maddy are watching from the doorway. We all hear Matt's bedroom door open and see Elaine holding Kitty in the crowded hallway. Everyone is overjoyed that Matt's back and appears to be okay.

Finally, Matt is able to talk and clearly says, "I'm okay, I'm okay." He turns to look out the window and I follow his gaze. The moon is no longer shining into the bathroom window as it's too low now to shine in the window. When he turns back around, he looks at me and I nod slightly to indicate I noticed too.

Matt now looks at everyone and says, "I'm going to change into some dry clothes." Everyone moves to give him space to leave the bathroom. When he stands though, I see he's wobbly so I go back to help him to his room and go inside with him. Once I close the door, he asks me, "How long was I gone?"

Full Moon Shadow

I reply, "A little over an hour." Matt hands me his wet clothes and then digs out dry ones from his dresser. I am surprised he seems so calm. "Is the Shadow Man going to leave us alone now? We were all so worried."

Matt nods and says, "He'll leave us alone now." But then he stops, looks at me and shrugs his shoulders. "I'll explain soon enough." He finishes dressing in dry clothes. He reaches into the pockets of his wet sweat pants that I'm holding and fishes out the cell phone which I notice is still in a baggie and the piece of jawbone which is no longer in the old sock. He pulls a blanket from his bed and places the two items in the folds of the blanket and drapes it over his arm.

As we walk into the hallway, I hear Elaine's percolator and smell coffee. I silently bless this sweet old lady and think of dropping Matt's wet clothes onto the hallway floor to run and get the desperately needed beverage. But with Matt by my side, I think that isn't the best option so I detour into the bathroom and put his drenched clothes in the tub with the wet towels. Kitty followed me into the bathroom so I pick her up. Before I turn to leave, I stop and look out the bathroom window into the now dark sky. Even though there is no longer a shadow on the hallway wall, I feel goosebumps on my arms walking by the now blank hallway wall.

I join the others in the living room. Matt is now on the couch with his mom and dad on either side of him. We are all enjoying hot coffee after the long night. Maddy and Darla are sitting on the floor in front of the couch. Elaine is on the recliner and mom is sitting in a kitchen chair by the recliner facing the couch. I sit on the floor next to Darla and put Kitty on the couch. She climbs into Matt's lap. Derek tells Matt, "We recorded you going into the shadow and then coming out. You were in there for 85 minutes." Derek holds up the phone and starts the playback and we all see Matt disappearing into the wall. I look at Darla and Maddy's faces and they both have their mouths open in amazement at what they see.

Full Moon Shadow

Derek stops the playback after Matt's disappearance and turns to Matt, "Can you give us a summary of what happened inside the shadow, please? Or perhaps you can playback the recording, if that will help."

Matt nods. "Wait, let me check if the voice memo is still on. I don't think I've turned it off yet." He pulls out the cell phone from under the blanket he has in his lap and takes it out of the baggie. He holds it up and we see it's still recording. He presses a few buttons and we hear what must me the Shadow Man's voice but it's hard to hear clearly. Matt turns up the volume:

> **Shadow Man:** *"So you decided to come and speak with me again."*
>
> **Matt:** *"Yes, I came to help."* His voice is muffled and then we hear Matt repeat himself: *"My name is Matt. I came back to find out what you need me to do for you. Please let me know how I can help."*
>
> **Shadow Man:** *"I want you to tell me why your people killed me. And why now, even after death, you do not let me rest in peace?"* We can tell he must be coming closer to Matt as is voice gets stronger with each word and he sounds very angry.

Matt stops the play back and looks around to see how the group is responding.

I look at Derek and Brenda; they look horrified. I look at the others and they are also wide eyed and shocked. No one asks Matt to continue the play back. Matt puts the phone down and explains what he learned from the Shadow Man in his own words.

"The Shadow Man is a Native American who was killed about 150 years ago by a white man. The Shadow Man's brother buried him next to a young oak tree in an open field. That field is now Aunt Leah's back yard and that young oak tree is the same huge beautiful valley oak that she had cut down four years ago because it was leaning towards the house and about to fall over. Leaning

Full Moon Shadow

Oak is what he calls himself because the tree he was buried next to was leaning slightly towards the northeast even then."

"He said his spirit first stirred when his grave was uncovered. That must have been when the tree was cut down and the stump ground down. Then his spirit was disturbed when part of his body was removed from his grave. That was when Aunt Leah found his jaw bone and put it in her house. He said that since his grave was disturbed by the removal of a bone, he can no longer be in peace. That is why he started coming during the full moon; he's been trying to tell someone that he wants to be reburied. Only then can he go back to the peaceful place he was in before his body was uncovered. He wants all of his body reburied together."

Matt now pulls out the piece of jaw bone he took with him into the shadow. "A group of men started shooting at several Native Americans when they refused to leave their tribal home. Leaning Oak managed to run quite far away but one man pursued and pushed him into a stream full of rushing water and storm debris. He landed on a log with his face and that is likely what broke his jaw. He told me when he managed to get to the side of the creek, his head and mouth were bleeding. His brother found him and pulled him out of the stream and they tried to walk to safety. As I mentioned, they didn't get very far before Leaning Oak died and his brother buried him next to an oak tree in what then was a vacant field." Matt nods his head in the direction of the back yard. Everyone's eyes are wide having heard these gruesome details.

Matt looks around the room and asks, "Any questions?" Mom surprises me and asks, "This time you came back all wet but last time, you were all dirty. I'm curious about the difference?"

"Last month I entered the shadow, we went to a dirt clearing surrounded by trees. I fell in the dirt that time. Today, we were in a meadow next to a fast-flowing stream and I didn't fall down. To take me back, after he encased me in his light, he ran and jumped with me in his arms into the stream. We were completely submerged in the water and when I re-emerged, I was alone in the hallway all wet." Mom looks white and murmurs thanks.

Full Moon Shadow

I ask Matt, "Where, or what was this, this realm you were in?"

Matt thinks for a minute and then says, "Leaning Oak described it as an intermittent place that is accessible only during the full moon. It's where spirits are allowed to communicate with the living to try to get things put right. As I mentioned, he wants to be reburied so he can rest in peace and that's why he's been haunting the house. He was very angry when he heard about the jawbone being removed from his grave. Lucky for me, he's not allowed to go back to the peaceful place if he hurts anyone; the spirits will not allow that. For that, I am very thankful.

* * *

It's almost 6 am when Elaine heads home and Mom gives Darla, Maddy and their bikes a ride home. Brenda falls asleep on the couch while Matt, Derek and I listen to the complete voice recording of Matt's time in the shadow in my room. The recording provided enough information without needing to ask Matt many questions. None of us really want to talk about it anymore. In fact, I doubt I will get any slept after hearing it.

Derek erases the video from his new phone and now Matt erases the voice memo too. Derek then asks me, "CJ, can you please take both phones and make sure the recordings are really gone and not saved on the cloud anywhere?" I nod. Matt and Derek both leave my room and I do as I was asked. Later, I find Derek lying back in the recliner with his eyes closed but I can tell he's still awake. Mom arrives soon after and asks if she can sleep in my bed. I go into Matt's room and we both lay on his bed fully clothed and eventually fall asleep as the sun is coming up.

CHAPTER 6: THE REST OF SPRING QUARTER, 2024

Matt

Even after being up all night, we are all up and eating breakfast by 10 am. Around 11 am, I call the police and tell them I found a human bone in my house. Within minutes, the police arrive and at first, it's not too bad. But within a couple of hours, a full out investigation begins. I give the police Aunt Leah's journal, her letter to me as well as the sketch I made of her yard work. Last night, I destroyed the hand written list of yard receipts as it had the notes about when Aunt Leah and Elaine saw the Shadow Man. If needed, I will give the police the past yard work receipts but they don't seem interested in that kind of information. I don't mention about Stan's yard work to remove the exposed roots and cover them up. Why get him involved unnecessarily?

What they DO want to know is why we didn't call them immediately when we found the jawbone. I say truthfully, "We weren't sure what to do. It was rather shocking, you know? My parents were in town for Picnic Day and we discussed it with them. They stayed here in Davis to help me figure out what was best to do about it. We considered several possible reasons a human bone could have ended up in my Aunt Leah's back yard." They just looked at me like I was crazy so I added, "Maybe long ago a coyote or a dog found the bone and buried it here. Who knows? But regardless, we just found it two days ago and decided it was best to call you." The police woman writes a note in her pad.

Full Moon Shadow

When a police car arrives at the house, neighbors are curious but respectful. But when more official vehicles arrive and a crime scene tent is put up in the backyard, the neighbors are no longer discrete and are hanging around watching and listening to learn what is going on. Elaine tells them all about our mystery object that we'd been searching for and that we found the bone by accident behind the bookcase just two days ago.

As we are interviewed repeatedly, we are very glad we have many truths we can tell the police. For example, we tell them about how we set up the bedroom for CJ and then found the jaw bone behind the bookcase. This makes dealing with the process a little bit easier. Needless to say, CJ and I don't go to classes on Wednesday as the police told us they might have more questions. Not sure we could have handled going to classes anyway with only having a couple of hours sleep.

By the second day, it is really a zoo at Aunt Leah's house. There are police officers, coroner's staff digging throughout the yard, and strangers looking through the windows, and crossing the police tape to come into the yard. The police, thankfully, get rid of these rubberneckers quickly. The one problem the police are fed up dealing with though, is Kitty as she keeps getting into the crime scene tent to help dig. I ask Elaine to keep her at her house and not let her outside to keep her out of the way. With all that is going on at the house, there's no way we could study or have any kind of privacy staying at Aunt Leah's house. That's why we are all staying in a motel.

Sally heads home on Thursday but mom and dad stay through the weekend and invite CJ, Elaine, Maddy and Darla to dinner the night before they head home. They want to tell us about the conference call we had with our family attorney. It was agreed that if it's confirmed that the body is a Native American, I will give the arrowhead and shells to the Native American Heritage Commission. We think it's likely they will bury the artifacts with Leaning Oak's body. We are all quiet for a few minutes thinking about this. Maddy tells us that sometimes Tribal Representatives perform a ceremony when remains are reburied. We all agree that this would be nice.

Elaine comes over to say goodbye to mom and dad before they head back to Berkeley. Kitty is in a cat carrier meowing pitifully in the back seat. I agreed with mom that it is best she permanently move to their house since my new apartment doesn't allow pets. Plus, Elaine doesn't really want to keep Kitty as she is scratching up all her doors trying to go back to Aunt Leah's house. I'm sad but know that I will at least see Kitty when I go home. Before they go, mom and dad tell us they're going to put Aunt Leah's house up for sale. I am fine with this decision and so is Elaine.

* * *

It takes over a month for the police investigation to conclude. They found the skeletal remains of a male Native American at the approximate age of 30. They estimate he died about 150 years ago. While the investigation was going on, my dad started quietly looking for an interested commercial buyer. Within weeks, they sold the house to a residential developer who plans to tear down the house and replace it with a fourplex. With the proceeds from the house sale, my parents made a large donation to both the Native American Heritage Commission and to a Native American Studies scholarship fund at UC Davis. My parents don't tell me how much, but they do say that the rest of the house sale proceeds were added to a trust fund Aunt Leah set up for me long ago. None of us were sad her house was gone as we know Aunt Leah herself would have said, "I'm not my house." We will always remember her.

In mid-May, I meet my parents at Aunt Leah's house to help sort through her boxes in the garage. Everything else from the house and garage is now gone. We each open a box and find inside several brown, shoebox-sized containers labeled with people's names. We start stacking the containers in neat piles until Mom finds one with her name. She pulls up a chair and opens the box. "Look, she wrote me a letter; it's dated 2009." She scans the letter and explains that Aunt Leah started sorting through her things when she retired and put them into these boxes for us to give out after she passed. "I'm so touched she did this." She looks a bit through the box and finds some jewelry, a scarf, many photos, and other keepsake items. I can see mom is moved by this and goes to get a tissue.

Later, when we find a box for Elaine, we call her and she comes right over. We have moved from the garage and are now sitting at the dining room table while Elaine opens her box. She insists that she wants to open it in front of us. She sets aside her letter to read later and then began looking deeper into the box. There's a stack of recipe cards tied together in a bundle that she pulls out first. "What in the world?" She gently unties the ribbon and picks up the top card. "It's my recipe for blueberry muffins." She turns the card over and finds an attached sticky note and she reads aloud:

> I tried making your recipe for blueberry muffins today. I thought I did everything right since I followed the recipe. I put it in the oven and set the timer for 20 minutes. I figured that was enough time for me to go water my rosebush. The next I know; my smoke alarm is going off. Well, the muffins were overdone to say the least and I never could get the black out of that muffin pan.

Elaine bursts out laughing! We all join in until we notice Elaine's laughter has stopped and she's now very sad. "I miss her so much." Mom hands her a tissue. "Leah, you were a great horticulturalist but a darn lousy baker!"

* * *

Once Elaine leaves, we go back to the garage to finish and my dad says, "I'm surprised there wasn't a box for you, Matt."

"Dad, remember..." But when I see his face, I know he's teasing me. I smile thinking of the boxes for me that CJ put in my room. I go back to my sorting but I can feel mom and dad looking at me so I look up. They're holding a letter out to me. I take it from them puzzled.

Full Moon Shadow

"Read the PS, Matt." Mom says pointing the bottom of the page:

"PS

Please let little Matty know that I have already saved so many things of his that I know they won't all fit into one little box. I'm sure there will be several boxes for him. I plan to write him his own letter when he's older. I hope I get a chance.

Also, I want to thank you both for allowing me so much time with him. He has brought so much joy to my life; I can't begin to describe it. Please give this to him to remember me by.

Love, Leah"

I look up and see my dad is holding out a small framed photograph. It shows Aunt Leah sitting on the swing seat with me in her lap. The swing is in motion and we are both smiling as big as could be.

* * *

After mom makes a list of all the people Aunt Leah left memory boxes for, she realizes she can no longer put off having a Celebration of Life for her. There are too many to invite to hold it at someone's house so the party venue is set for the UC Davis Alumni Center, the day after finals. Over 100 people attend; neighbors, former colleagues and students, and, of course, family. The luncheon is catered by Aunt Leah's favorite Mexican restaurant. Cara and Elaine provide desserts, mom and Sally, the decorations. I help by placing flowering potted plants at the entrance and smaller ones on each table. I know Aunt Leah would've liked that as she always preferred living plants to cut flowers.

There is even an unexpected guest; the Plant Sciences Department Chair attends and announces they are dedicating a bench to Aunt Leah at the UC Davis Arboretum to be placed in the Redwood Grove.

Full Moon Shadow

CJ

The next day after the Shadow Man confrontation, the house is a zoo with the police here. Matt and his parents are being grilled but lucky for mom and I, they only ask us a few questions. That was okay as the two of us called about the apartment, went to see the place and started the paperwork. We can move in May 1st.

To avoid the craziness at the house, I share a motel room with Matt. Thankfully, it was a different motel from where his parents are staying so we could come and go without feeling like we are being supervised. Over dinner one night with Darla and Maddy, we all agree that we never want to talk about the Shadow Man again. We are glad to be back in classes and can focus now knowing that it's in the past.

Once we moved into the apartment, Matt and I had an awesome time. I did a lot of cooking for the two of us; I'm getting better all the time. Matt even asked for me to show him how to cook something for Maddy's 19th birthday, May 10. It was an easy meal; meatballs, pasta and sauce with a salad. He did good though and said she was impressed. Then Darla surprised me and took me to dinner in San Francisco for my 19th birthday, May 25. It was nice to be in the city as it was foggy there. Davis is a bit too hot in the spring for my taste.

The Celebration of Life for Leah is the first time I see Brenda and Derek after Matt and I moved into our apartment. They look much more relaxed now. She and my mom have a few too many glasses of wine together and are giggling a lot towards the end. I think it is nice they have become friends.

Mom wants me to move home for the summer. She thinks I should get a job to gain some work experience and start learning to manage a budget. I'm okay with that. Her divorce will be final soon and she's selling our house. I have to go through my room and all that – UGH! She's looking for a new house and wants to find one that has a professional grade kitchen.

Full Moon Shadow

Matt and I talk about what we want to do in the fall and we decide to not be roommates. We are still friends but just want to broaden our circles. Similarly, Darla and I break up at the end of spring quarter. It was mutual this time and for the best. I am the kind of guy that really likes my time alone and it is hard for me to stay too long in any relationship.

It is cool that Matt's parents were able to sell Aunt Leah's house and that it's being replaced with a fourplex. It likely would have been impossible to sell it to a family after a body was found in the backyard. It's better there will be something different in its place. I go by from time to time to see if they've started construction. Who am I kidding? I like to chat with the neighbors. Of course, they all ask about Matt. I think they're a bit surprised I'm the one that stops by instead of him. I shrug my shoulders and change the subject. Over coffee, Elaine tells me that Matt meets her for coffee downtown every now and then.

When I think about my time living in the house with Matt, I did like the space and neighborhood. But the upkeep was a lot of work, especially the yard. Matt used to ask me to help him with stuff like mow the lawn, rake, things like that. Definitely, not my thing. I'm happier in an apartment with less upkeep, no yard work, and especially, no ghosts.

EPILOGUE: THREE YEARS LATER

Matt

I graduated from UC Davis with a Bachelor of Arts degree in Communication! I was accepted to graduate school at an Ivy League college back east and started in the fall. I'm sure you're curious, what happened to my majoring in Plant Sciences? Well, I realized during my second year that Plant Sciences wasn't my passion. I had selected that major mostly to please Aunt Leah. Communications is really my passion. I want to be a voice for others that don't have one. I'm still trying to figure out exactly what that means. I guess that my time in the spirit world made me realize there are lots of people, animals, etc. that need someone to speak for them. I'm hoping graduate school will help me figure out how best to do this.

In case you're wondering, Maddy and I dated for several months after that eventful April. However, she never could shake what happened at Aunt Leah's house; it was more than she could handle. She told me that she was naïve thinking that going into a shadow wasn't a big deal. Once she saw the jawbone though, she realized how real and dangerous it could be and that got to her. She regretted being at the house when I went into the shadow and felt that I kind of talked her into it. That didn't help our relationship much either. Even though I apologized and she knows it all turned out okay, she needed time away from Davis and from me to heal. She transferred to UC Riverside the middle

146

of her second year. I told her I understood. After all, when I allow myself to remember what happened when I lived in Aunt Leah's house, I shudder. It was a very troubling experience. I'm just glad that I have so many good memories with Aunt Leah that are not tied to her house.

I keep thinking about how Maddy and I stayed in touch for a few months after she transferred. However, when we each began dating other people, it was awkward to still be communicating so we drifted apart. While I had some nice girlfriends the last couple of years, no relationship lasted very long. I wonder if Maddy had better luck. She certainly deserves someone special.

I've been in graduate school for a couple of weeks now and completed my first week of classes and find myself a bit lonely. I have no plans for the weekend and wonder how to fill my time. I'd like to spend some time with my roommate to get better acquainted but he's gone this weekend. I sit down on a park bench and look out at the beautiful fall day. I flip through my contacts thinking I will call an old friend to say hello. I just talked to CJ a couple of days ago, so someone else this time. Maddy comes to mind again and I wonder if her cell number is still the same. It would be interesting to see how's she's doing. I'm just about to push the call button when I hear a voice from behind me.

"Matt, is that you?!" The voice, it sounds so familiar, could it be? I stand up and turn around and there she is, in person! I drop my phone in surprise and reach out and impulsively hug her. Maddy hugs me back, then joins me on the bench and we talk for a long time. It is so great to see her again.

Full Moon Shadow

CJ

This summer, I graduated from UC Davis with my BS degree in Physics and Astronomy - woohoo! I think back to that first year and how hard it was to get my bearings. I'm so grateful I had both my mom and Matt to help me figure it all out. Now I'm at Stanford University, CA working on my PhD. Maybe I will be a professor when I'm done, who knows? I think I've grown a lot while in college. Matt used to think I was so cool because I got good grades, didn't participate in class discussions, group projects, and in general, didn't talk much. But I never told Matt that I used to be afraid to share my ideas with others unless, of course, *I knew I was right*. Now I really enjoy discussions and debates, especially about science.

I just got a call from Matt a few days ago. Turns out, Maddy is going to the same graduate school he's attending and they're dating again. I'm so happy to hear that as the two of them seem to balance each other out. When they were together at Davis, he was calmer and less talkative. Maddy filled the quiet with her confidence and joy. Who knows? Maybe someday I will find someone that fits me like they fit each other.

You might want to know what happened with my mom. Her divorce from Mitch was final over two years ago. She's still single and I think it's a good thing that she doesn't want to rush into a new relationship. At first, she really struggled and told me she was lonely. However, she called me a few months later and told me that her alone time was allowing her to focus on what she really wanted to do with her life. Just last month, she called me to announce that she's cut back her counseling hours for her new venture; she's offering personal cooking lessons in her new home. GO MOM! I know she will do well since she taught me to cook when I didn't even know how to fry an egg.

So far, I'm enjoying Stanford a lot. But I was getting panicked after I got accepted trying to find a place to live. Housing is very hard to find and exorbitantly expensive. Just when I was thinking I would have to live far away and deal with a long commute, a friend told me about a house near campus that rents primarily to graduate students. I clicked on the link she sent me and read: *"A beautiful house and yard..."* I inwardly groaned remembering how much I dislike yard work. I hold my breath and read the rest of the sentence: *"...all maintained by the property manager."* Great!

Only one more thing I had to check before I could make the commitment. I made an appointment to look at the room that same day. It's an older three-story home that has been remodeled to rent out rooms. I asked to see the room; I was very happy to find out that the windows do not face the west. That means, no full moon shadow to worry about in THIS house. I signed the lease with no reservations.

The End

www.ingramcontent.com/pod-product-compliance
Lightning Source LLC
Chambersburg PA
CBHW060827120626
46557CB00001B/398